Hey Boris," said Ape Face. "The Mets are ahead two uns. Don't you want to watch?"

"No," said Boris crossly.

I said, "Yes you do, Boris. You most definitely do. First, read this." I pointed to the place in *TV Guide* vhere it said under Saturday: NY Mets–Cincinnati Reds, live, Shea Stadium.

"So?"

"So now look at the TV screen: The Mets and the Cincinnati Reds at Shea Stadium. The Mets are still playing the Montreal Expos today. Doesn't that strike you as odd?"

"So what? It's probably a rerun."

"No, it's live," said Ape Face happily.

"Tell him, Ape Face," I said. "Start at the beginning and tell him the whole thing."

READ ALL THE FREAKY FRIDAY STORIES!

Freaky Friday

Summer Switch

A Billion for Boris (*also known as* ESP TV)

MARY RODGERS

A Billion for Boris

Also known as ESP TV

HarperTrophy®
An Imprint of HarperCollinsPublishers

A Billion for Boris

Printed in the United States of America. For information address HarperCollins Children's Books, a division of HarperCollins Publishers, 1350 Avenue of the Americas, New York, NY 10019.

Library of Congress Cataloging-in-Publication Data
Rodgers, Mary.
A billion for Boris / Mary Rodgers.
p. cm.
Summary: When they discover an old TV that plays tomorrow's programs, fourteen-year-old Annabel and her fifteen-year-old friend Boris try to use it to help mankind and earn money to renovate Boris's eccentric mother.
ISBN 0-06-051230-X (pbk.)
[1. Television—Fiction. 2. Mothers—Fiction.] I. Title.
PZ7.R6155 Bi 1974 74-3586
[Fic]—dc20 CIP
AC

Revised Harper Trophy edition, 2003

Visit us on the World Wide Web!
www.harperchildrens.com

This book is dedicated to my small sons, Adam and Alec, without whom I was finally able to finish it.

115 C.P.W.
N.Y., N.Y., 10023

Barron University
Dept. of ESP and Parapsychology
Greensboro, N.C.

Dear Sirs:

Enclosed please find a detailed account of a most unusual experience recently undergone by me, my brother, and a friend of mine who lives upstairs in our apartment building. This experience doesn't exactly fall into the category of ESP, but it was definitely a psychic phenomenon of some sort or other so I thought you might like to have a record of it for your archives. I also thought maybe you'd have a logical explanation for the whole thing, but if you don't, I'll certainly understand.

In any case, I'd appreciate hearing from you at your earliest possible convenience.

Very sincerely yours,
Annabel Andrews

P.S. Rest assured that every word of the following document is the *absolute verbatim truth*! I say this only because I am a person to whom peculiar things happen from time to time but nobody ever believes me. Last year, for instance, there was a Friday in February when I woke up and found out I'd turned into my mother. It was a pretty freaky Friday, and not one I'd want to repeat—but that's not the point. The point is, when the going got rough and I needed help, I couldn't find anybody to believe me. I told three cops and my trusted (but not very trusting) friend who lives upstairs, and they all thought I was crazy. Granted, it was a rather bizarre occurrence, but compared to what you're about to read, it positively reeked with credibility. Anyway, I'm counting on the fact that you people *will* believe me, because if *you* don't, who will?

Very, *very* sincerely yours,
A.A

Preliminary Information

BEFORE I DO ANYTHING ELSE, I'd better list some basic facts about myself, my brother, and my friend.

BASIC FACTS ABOUT MYSELF

I am fourteen years old, five foot four and still growing (I hope). I have brown eyes, brown hair (mousy), and I weigh a hundred and fifteen pounds before breakfast. (If you don't want to be depressed, before breakfast is the only time to get on a scale.)

My parents, Ellen Jean Benjamin Andrews and William Waring Andrews, my brother Ape Face (on the birth certificate it says Benjamin but to me he's Ape Face), our dog Max, and I live in an apartment on Central Park West in New York City. I'm in the ninth grade at the Barden School where I do pretty well when I try and, according to my teachers, "surprisingly well" even when I don't. The subjects I try at are

English, current events, history, and biology.

Home economics, which we have once a week, I don't try at. I'm going to be a journalist when I grow up, and my husband will simply have to accept the fact that I don't cook, clean, or iron shirts. Not that there's anything demeaning about housework, but unlike my mother, I'm not the domestic type.

You know what she said to me the other day? She said, "Annabel, you are an incorrigible slob."

I said, "No, I'm not, Ma. You and I have different standards, that's all."

"Yes," she said. "Mine are higher."

Oh well, maybe now that she's started taking courses full-time at Columbia University, she'll be forced to lower hers. I hope so, because except for fights about my neatness, I would say we have an excellent relationship.

My father is an account executive at an advertising agency called Joffert and Jennings. Last year, he handled New Improved Fosphree; but then the EPA discovered it was killing all the fish in the Schoharie Reservoir, and the product was taken off the market. Just as well. The company used to send us a ton of the stuff free every month and it turned all the laundry gray. Personally, I was hoping he'd get assigned to a candy account—free chocolate bars every month would have been sensational—but instead he got Merrill Lynch which is a big brokerage firm and doesn't send you anything.

Generally speaking, I have an excellent relationship with my father, too. The only trouble with him is he works too hard and worries about money too much. Other than that, he's a neat guy and fairly unsquare, considering his age. (Thirty-nine.)

Basic Facts About Ape Face

He is seven years old, four feet something-or-other and still growing (I assume). He has blue eyes, ash-blond hair (but in a couple of years it'll *turn* mousy, I'll bet), and I don't know what he weighs. All I know is he's one of those kids who eats everything that's put in front of him and then some and never gets fat. He must be shot with luck.

Incidentally, in case you're curious about his nickname, I started calling him that the day he came home from the hospital. I was six and a half, and at that age if you're planning on a sister and what you get instead is a male monkey, you're not inclined to mince words.

"It's got a face like an ape," I said, giving it a cautious poke. "What's it called?"

"Benjamin. Or Ben, if you like that better," said my mother, trying to be accommodating.

"I like Ape Face better."

"Well, he won't," said my mother firmly. "It'll only make him mad."

But it didn't. That's what's so funny. I only recently found out that all those years I was calling him Ape Face to make him mad, I was only making my mother mad. Ape Face *loved* it. I think he feels it gives him a kind of macho authority. Sometimes he lopes around the apartment saying things like, "Annabel, you're not supposed to put your feet on the coffee table," and when I say, "Who says?" he says, "The Ape says," and pounds his chest like a twelve-foot gorilla. Other times, he just stands there embarrassing me in front of my friends by pushing his lower lip out with his tongue, scratching his ribs with his left paw, picking imaginary cooties out of his hair and eating them with the right paw, and grunting, *"Unh, unh, unh."* It's really disgusting. I should have stuck with the name Ben. Or Benjie. Actually, when I get mad enough, that's exactly what I do call him and it makes him furious. Shows what mothers know.

All in all, he's not too bad; I just wish he weren't so *tidy*. He's tidy about his clothes, tidy about toothpaste tubes (always squeezes from the bottom and puts the cap back on), and if you really want to see something, you should see his tiny, tidy room. It's only ten by twelve and in it he has managed to fit: twenty-seven stuffed animals, a fleet of Dinky cars, a toy chest full of assorted Lego pieces, a large Childcraft Work Bench, a toolbox of Baby Ben innards, and a pachinko set—tidily. My room is much bigger but it usually looks like the aftermath of a Macy's bargain-basement sale. I don't know how he does it.

In the old days, I used to think he did it just to show me up; but now that I've gotten more tolerant, I've decided he can't help being the way he is. And anyway, he's improving; twice this week he's forgotten to wash out his bathtub ring.

Basic Facts About Boris

Boris Harris is fifteen, five foot ten (definitely still growing—otherwise, why would his hands and feet be so enormous?), has hazel eyes, chestnut hair (beautiful), and probably weighs around one forty-five.

He lives upstairs in an apartment which until recently I'd never seen, with a mother I'd never met, even though I'd known him for umpteen years and been good friends with him for over a year. Can you *imagine*? His mother was a complete mystery. All I knew was that she was divorced from his father (who had then died when Boris was eight) and hated to cook—that much he'd told me. But I didn't know anything else because he didn't talk about her often. When he did, it wasn't very complimentary.

For instance, one night last year when he was having dinner in our apartment, my mother said, "Boris, I've never met your mother. Tell me, what's she like?"

Boris stared at his plate for a second and then

flatly announced, "By buther is a crub," which translated loosely means "I don't like her much."

"I beg your pardon?" inquired my mother politely.

"Dever bide, Bisses Adrews. Forget I said it," said Boris.

It was then I finally realized why it was that whenever Boris came down from upstairs, he always sounded as though he had a cold for the first few minutes and then the symptoms cleared up. He was allergic to his mother! (I'm happy to report that he seems to have outgrown this; it almost never happens anymore.)

The same evening, I also realized that Boris's real name was actually Morris. But I went on calling him Boris anyway—because he was used to it by then, and so was I.

Other basic facts about Boris are: He's a grade ahead of himself in school and still gets all A's. He says his school is probably easier than mine but I doubt it. I think he's just incredibly smart. And modest.

He has a super sense of humor.

He wins almost every argument we have, and we have quite a few. It isn't that we don't get along or anything, we just like to argue for the fun of it.

But the most important basic fact about Boris is that I love him. And although he hasn't exactly said so, I think he loves me, too.

How It All Began

It was a Saturday afternoon in February. The weather was unbelievably repulsive; rain mixed with sleet, slippery sidewalks, icy wind that turned your umbrella inside out—the kind of day that makes you wish your dog was paper trained because he doesn't want to go out any more than you do. Especially a dog like our basset, Max, who's too lazy to go out even if it's a sunny morning in spring.

So anyway, that's the kind of afternoon it was. Boris and I were playing records in the living room, my mother was in the study doing her homework, my father was out to lunch with a client from Chicago, and Ape Face was being a pain in the neck. For about the eleventh time in the last half hour, he stood in the doorway of the living room.

"Annabel," he began.

"Are you here again? What do you want now?"

"Would you play me a game of Crazy Eights?"

"No."

"Boris, would you?"

"Thanks, anyway."

"Well, won't somebody play *some*thing with me? There's nothing to do around here."

"Watch television."

"I'm not allowed. Only *Sesame Street, The Electric Company,* or *Mister Rogers' Neighborhood,* and they're not on."

"Get Mom to invite a friend over for you."

"She tried. Nobody's mother wants to go out in all this rain and stuff."

"I don't blame them. What about a friend in the building?"

"I don't *have* a friend in the building. My only friend was George and he moved to the country. *You* know that."

"As a matter of fact, I did not know that. Listen, I'm sorry your friend moved to the country and I'm sorry you're so bored, but there isn't a thing I can do about it. So if you wouldn't mind getting out of here and stop bothering us—*now.* Scram! Go amuse yourself. Take apart a Baby Ben clock or something."

I figured that should occupy him for at least an hour.

Ape Face sighed. "Okay," he said.

A hot ten minutes later, he was back again. I tried to control my temper.

"Finished already? My, that was speedy of you!" Much too speedy if you ask me. I shot Boris a look of despair. Boris took over.

"Ben, old boy, I have a great idea for you. Why don't you try putting the clock back together?"

"I already did."

"Oh," said Boris, nonplussed. "Congratulations."

"It was easy," said Ape Face. "I've done it a million times. There's nothing in my whole room I haven't done a million times. So Annabel, I was just wondering . . ." he said hesitantly.

"Wondering what?"

"Are you using your hair dryer right now?"

"Obviously not. Why?"

"I want to take it apart," Ape Face said.

"Oh you do, do you! Well, that's just altogether tough luck. It's a brand-new dryer and I'm not about to let you muck around with it. You'll wreck it up."

"Please?"

"*No!*" I shouted. "Now get out of here before I kill you!"

"Wait a minute," said Boris. "I think I have something that might interest you, Ape Face. In our apartment there's an old TV set. It's absolutely beyond repair—hasn't worked for years—but it has a lot of tubes and wires and parts you'd have fun fiddling around with. How does that sound?"

Ape Face was thrilled. "That sounds great!"

"I thought so. I'll tell you what: Seeing as it's no good to anyone but a mechanical nut like you, I'll sell it to you for a very low price."

"How much price?" asked Ape Face anxiously.

"Fifty cents."

Ape Face was crestfallen. "I don't have fifty cents. I spent all my money on Wacky Packs. Couldn't I go upstairs to your house and you just lend me the use of the set for a couple of hours?"

"No," said Boris firmly. "You going upstairs is not a good idea. But even if you don't have the money, I'd be happy to bring it down to you now anyway; and you could pay me later. Okay?"

"Okay," said Ape Face. "There's just one thing. I hope you're not going to get mad at me—but if the set's no good, why do I have to pay you fifty cents for it?" I must say, he had a point there. It did seem rather greedy.

Boris looked faintly annoyed. "The effort of lugging it down here is worth at least fifty cents. Besides, it's a seller's market. In other words, I've got what you want, and whether or not anyone else wants it is immaterial. You do want it, don't you?"

"Oh yes," said Ape Face.

"All right, then. It's a deal. Annabel, you're the witness."

"Fine by me," I said. "I just hope he doesn't electrocute himself."

"Oh, don't be silly," said Ape Face scornfully. "I know all about electricity. I know better than that. I wouldn't plug it in while I was working on it—only when it was all fixed up."

"That'll be the day," said Boris flippantly.

Friday, April 12

It was my fourteenth birthday. There was nothing particularly significant about it except that it was the nicest one I'd ever had. Its not being a school night, my parents took me and Boris to Gallagher's Steak House, and after that they let Boris take me alone to The Bitter End in the Village, where Boris finally presented me with the package he'd been lugging around all night. From the large size of it, I was prepared for the disappointing fact that it couldn't be anything personal like a ring or a bangle, but I was not prepared for anything as impersonal as a pair of walkie-talkies.

"Boy, Boris, that's got to be the most original present anybody ever gave anybody." I am nothing if not truthful.

"Useful, too," said Boris, obviously quite pleased with himself. Useful for what? I wondered.

"Oh, I'll bet. And even if they weren't, they're so attractive—those nice leather cases."

"Glad you like them," said Boris, putting one walkie-talkie back in the carton and shoving the other into the pocket of his parka.

"Hey!" I protested. "Where are you going with that? What am I going to do with *one* walkie-talkie?"

"One for you, one for me; these things'll transmit through steel, cement, carpets, the works—we'll use them instead of the telephone."

"But what's the matter with the telephone?"

"Too expensive," said Boris.

"Weren't the walkie-talkies expensive? They *look* expensive."

"Sure, but at the rate you and I talk to each other, I figure they'll amortize themselves in two and a half months."

"Since when did you get so economy-minded?"

"Since five days ago. My mother said if I didn't stop tying up her phone, she'd have my own phone installed and make me pay for it. This way is going to be a lot cheaper and we won't ever have to depend on the phone again."

When I got home and thought it all over, I decided Boris was a very practical person. I also decided that under certain circumstances, a walkie-talkie was more personal than a bangle. After all, bangles you could give to a thousand girls and none of them (including me) would be the wiser; but a walkie-talkie-for-two constituted a definite commitment to only one girl. And I was it. So I gave it a quick kiss, put it under my pillow, and went to sleep.

Saturday, April 13

BEEP, BEEP, BEEP. "Testing one two three four. This is Boris calling Annabel. Are you there, Annabel? If you are there, push the right-hand button and say something. Roger, over, and out."

I groped under the pillow for the walkie-talkie, pushed the right-hand button, and said, "What time is it?"

"You've got the wrong button, Annabel. I repeat: the *wrong button*. You've been pushing the signal button, which beeps." (You're telling me it beeps!) "The right-hand button is for talking, push the right-hand button. Roger, over, and out."

"I *am* pushing the right-hand button," I said grumpily. I wasn't, I was pushing the left-hand button—but it was too early to argue. Maybe his walkie-talkie was facing the other way.

"That's better. I hear you now. But not very well.

You're coming through muffled." I took the walkie-talkie out of its leather case.

"Better now?" I inquired.

"Much," said Boris.

"Say, Boris," I yawned, "what time is it?"

"Seven thirty."

I pushed the talk button and groaned loudly.

"I didn't wake you, did I? I thought you were an early riser."

"Mondays through Fridays I'm an early riser. Out of necessity, not preference. Saturdays and Sundays I'm a late riser."

"Gee, Annabel, I'm sorry," said Boris. "I assumed you'd be up and if you weren't, you wouldn't hear the signal."

"Sleeping through beeping is a virtual impossibility. I could have heard it in Anchorage, Alaska. Anyway, never mind. What's it like out?" My room faces west on an alley and the rest of the apartment faces either west or north. The only way to find out what to wear is to get down on the street and sample the air. By that time, it's usually too late to go back up and change into something else. Boris's apartment faces south and east; if the sun was out, he'd know about it.

"Gorgeous. Not a cloud in the sky, warm—according to my thermometer, forty-eight degrees. You couldn't ask for a better day. Want to go biking in the park?"

"Can't. My mother's going to the library to do some research. She's paying me to baby-sit Ape Face."

"Bring him along and I'll split the fee with you. He knows how to bike, doesn't he?"

"Not too well. Besides, knowing him, he'll want to go to the zoo."

"To visit his friends, I suppose."

"What friends? What do you mean?"

"Chimps, orangutans, purple-bottomed baboons . . . forget it. I was just being funny."

"Oh, is that what you were being? I thought you were being stupid."

"Okay, Annabel. I obviously got you at a bad time. Check with you later. Roger, over, and out." When Boris is hurt he doesn't say much—he just turns off. For a scrappy person like me, it's a maddening technique, but when we talked about it once, he said it was his way of coping. He said he learned to do it years ago when his parents used to use him for a football in their fights.

I beeped him back. After three or four minutes, I decided he was either sulking or out of earshot.

"Yeah," he said finally.

"What took you so long? Couldn't you hear me? This is Annabel."

"No kidding. Of course I heard you. So did my mother. When you disturb *her* at seven thirty in the morning she's even more charming than you. If I don't get her some coffee fast, she'll throw something at me, so if you don't mind, I'll sign off now. Roger . . ."

"Wait a minute, Boris. I just wanted to say I was sorry for snapping at you."

"Better you than my mother. What does the word 'Good-bye' mean to you? Roger, over, and out."

I wanted like anything to ask Boris to go to the zoo with me and the Ape, but after what he said about his mother, I didn't dare beep him again.

Not a very auspicious beginning for a day.

By ten thirty, my mother had left for the library, my father had left for the office to take care of some odds and ends of paper work, and I started getting dressed to take Ape Face to the zoo. Forty-eight degrees and sunny? Good. I could wear my new boots (birthday present from my mother), my new turtleneck sweater (from my father), my new secondhand Eisenhower jacket (from my friend Virginia—she got it at the thrift shop across the street from school), and my most treasured, old, soft, threadbare pair of Cloroxed blue jeans.

"Hey, Ape Face," I yelled. "Come here a second."

Ape Face appeared, still in his pajamas.

"Ta-dah!" I said, spreading my arms out and turning around for inspection. "How do you like me?"

Ape Face didn't seem quite sure. He looked me up and down and then said, "Where are we going?"

"To the zoo. I thought you wanted to go to the zoo."

"I do. I love the zoo."

"Well, what's the matter then?" Ape Face looked me up and down some more.

"Are you going to be warm enough? No hat, no gloves or anything? It's going to snow, you know."

"Don't be ridiculous," I said. "It's forty-eight degrees out and sunny."

"But later it's going to snow."

"You're cuckoo. I never heard of such a cuckoo thing!"

Ape Face shrugged. "Are those the new boots Mom gave you?"

"Yes. Super, aren't they."

"Waterproof?"

"No, dummy. Waterproof boots are clumpy and cloddy. These are thin and delicate. Finest Italian leather."

"They're going to get roond in the snow."

"The word is *ru*-ined, not roond, and they're not; because it's *not going to snow*! Hurry up and get dressed and stop bugging me about the weather."

Ordinarily, Ape Face is a fairly snappy dresser (by which I mean *quick* snappy as opposed to groove snappy), but twenty minutes later, there was no sign of him.

"What's taking you so long?" I shouted. "I've been waiting for hours."

"Coming," he answered. He didn't have to tell me

he was coming; I could hear him coming: An inexorable *schlup-schlup-schlup,* accompanied by *scrawk*-pause-*scrawk*-pause-*scrawk.* By now, I was prepared for practically anything. Which was fortunate, because what hove into view blew my mind. The Abominable Snowman himself, in Mighty-Mac, ski pants, scarf, mittens, galoshes (*schlup-schlup*), and a three-foot Flexible Flyer attached to a long rope (*scrawk*-pause-*scrawk*).

"Listen, you idiot fathead, if you think I'm going out on the street with you dressed like that on a day like this, you're out of your idiot fat head!"

The fact that I was absolutely incoherent with rage didn't seem to have the slightest effect on him. "You're getting paid a dollar twenty-five to baby-sit me to the zoo."

"Dragging a large sled over dry land all the way to Sixty-Fourth Street and back was not included in the bargain."

"I'll drag my own sled. Getting it home'll be easier anyway."

"You'll look like a horse's ass. Everybody'll laugh at you."

"Not when it snows, they won't. They'll laugh at *you.*"

So down to the zoo we went, with Ape Face *schlup*ing and *scrawk*ing and me six paces behind pretending I'd never seen him before in my life.

At two forty-five, that selfsame Saturday afternoon, April 13th, a freak blizzard hit the tri-state area! Within an hour and a half, while Ape Face was serenely communing with his relatives in the house of large primates (and I was holding my nose and wondering how come more and more people kept leaving until we were the only ones there), the temperature dropped twenty-five degrees, the wind velocity rose to near gale proportions, and six inches of snow covered the ground. Unbeknownst to me, of course. By four fifteen when we finally emerged, the entire zoo was totally deserted, and Central Park was a howling winter wonderland. Making our way home was going to be about as hazardous as marching across Antarctica.

I'll say one thing for my brother, though. He knows when to keep his mouth shut. Maybe it was only self-preservation—maybe he kept his mouth shut so the snow wouldn't blow in and drown him—but not once, in the whole hour it took us to get back, did he say, "I told you so." He did say, "I knew getting the sled home would be easier," but when I snarled, "Naturally it's easier. You're sitting on it and I'm pulling it across Sheep Meadow," he clammed up immediately.

Ape Face survived our little adventure unscathed. A slightly chapped chin where his wool scarf had rubbed, but otherwise toasty warm and contented. I, on the other hand, had to consign my beautiful new boots to the garbage and my frostbitten self to bed because I'd caught a revolting cold. In fact, two hours later, when I got around to beeping Boris to tell him what had happened, I already sounded so adenoidal he asked me if I was developing an allergy to *my* mother. Ha ha!

What he didn't ask me was how Ape Face could have known about the freak blizzard. I guess at the time it didn't seem significant. I was so glad to be home and warm, it didn't seem significant to me either. But it was—very. Because although we didn't know it at the time, IT had begun to happen.

Thursday, April 18

FIVE DAYS LATER, my mother, needlessly consumed with guilt about going to college while I honked and snorted, had decided to stay home and look after me. I told her it was ridiculous; I was perfectly all right. I had my box of Kleenex Man-Sized Tissues, my nose spray, my vaporizer, the portable Sony—what more could I want?

"Suppose you get hungry?" she asked doubtfully.

"I won't. My taste buds are shot and I'm full up on phlegm."

My mother looked faintly ill. "Annabel, please." She's not as medically oriented as I am.

"Anyway, Ma, the cleaning lady comes today, doesn't she? If I need anything, I can ask Mattie. Go on, now. If you miss classes, you'll get behind."

"No," she said. "It would make me uncomfortable. I keep feeling if I'd stayed home yesterday and the day before, you'd be all better by now."

"Rot!"

"Nevertheless . . ." she said. "Call me if you need me. I'll be around." Either I was sicker than I thought (pneumonia? pleurisy?), or else she was simply looking for an excuse to cut school. Maybe that's it, I thought drowsily. Like daughter, like mother. With that, I drifted off to sleep.

Eight hours later I woke up. My mother was sitting in a chair near the window, reading a tome.

"That was quite some nap you had there. I was beginning to worry. How do you feel?"

"Terrific." I blew a quart of wonderfulness out of my nose and heaved the Kleenex at the wastebasket. Missed.

"Why is it," she said, retrieving the nasty thing with two dainty fingers, "why is it that you're on the first basketball team at school but you can't hit the broad side of a barn at home?"

"Maybe it's a question of incentive. At school you get points for making a basket." She laughed and moved the basket closer to the bed.

"There's Daddy," she said.

"Where?"

"I heard the door slam." (All mothers have phenomenal hearing.) "Now, he's making a drink. Make me one, too," she called. "Now he's on his way in." She took her glasses off.

"Hi there, sweetie, how are you feeling?" Dad leaned down to kiss me.

"Wouldn't, if I were you. You'll catch the plague."

"I'll take my chances," he said, planting one on my forehead and moving over to my mother.

"Now you're going to give it to her," I said.

"She'll take her chances, too, won't you?" he said, planting one on her mouth.

"Sure," she said. Not that she had any choice in the matter since he'd already done it.

Now that the evening greetings were over, my mother began what I call The Daily News Roundup. This always intrigues me because although my parents are crazy about each other—I'm positive of that—neither one seems terribly interested in what the other one is doing. But they always ask anyway—out of politeness, I guess.

"How was your day?" said my mother.

"Pretty good. I had a two-hour meeting with Marc Adams and Grantly Harding. If Cavendish buys it, we're going to get into the television bag. Then I had lunch at Nino's with Parks to discuss . . ."

"I don't know how you can discuss anything in that place. It's so noisy," said my mother.

"They know me there and the food's edible," said my father, happy to be sidetracked. His part of the recital was over; now it was her turn.

"And how was *your* day?"

"Fascinating," she said. Since there's obviously nothing fascinating about spending your day in the company of a zonked-out kid, what she really meant was dull, but the irony eluded my father.

"That's good. Can I do anything for you? Get you anything?"

"No thanks." You know, it's interesting: If my mother offers to do something or get something, my father takes her up on it. If my father offers, my mother invariably says "No, thanks," and does it or gets it herself. Partly because it's easier—he never knows where anything is—and partly because her feminine consciousness hasn't been raised as much as mine has. When I grow up, Boris will have to know where things are; as a journalist who travels frequently, I may not always be around to show him.

"You could get me something, Daddy," I said brightly.

"I could?" His face was a study in incredulity.

"I'm starving." Which was true, as a matter of fact.

"Oh," he said. Now his face was a study in bewilderment and nervousness combined. "Well, uh . . ." He looked over at my mother.

"I'll do it, darling. What do you feel like eating, Annabel?"

"Just soup. Plain chicken noodle soup." My mother got to her feet. Dad put out a restraining hand. "Stay put," he said magnanimously. "I can make soup. Anybody can make soup. Pheasant under glass, no; soup, yes. I'll be back in a minute."

He was back in a minute, empty handed. Ma and I grinned at each other.

"I can't find any soup," he said helplessly. "Mattie must have switched all the cabinets around."

"No, she didn't," said Ma. "The soup's where it's always been: in the shallow cabinet by the kitchen door."

"It's not. I looked in there." Ma exhaled a sigh of irritation and wordlessly took off down the hall.

A minute later, she was back. "That's funny," she said sheepishly. "I can't find it either."

"Ha!" said Dad.

"Ha nothing," she said indignantly. "There were at least a dozen cans there yesterday. I put them there myself, *yesterday*. Because yesterday was the day I went to the A&P, remember, Annabel?"

"Yes, that's right."

"And they had a nice sale on Aunt Ethel's Quik 'n Easy Soup—twelve to a customer. I bought two mushroom, two tomato, two sorrel, and six chicken noodle for Annabel. Remember, Annabel? I fixed you some when I came home."

"Right. There should be eleven cans left."

"Good thinking!" said my father. He loves to tease me about my math. I stuck my tongue out at him. My mother wasn't in the mood for horseplay.

"Stop it, you two. I want to get to the bottom of this. What happened to those cans of soup?"

"Beats me," said Dad. "You don't suppose Mattie would . . ." he was too embarrassed to finish the sentence. I should hope so!

"She certainly wouldn't," I said. "She'd never take a thing out of this house unless we gave it to her. Ma, why don't you ask the Ape? Maybe he took them to school. At Thanksgiving, they ask us to donate canned goods for the poor and needy of St. James Parish."

"Annabel, this is not Thanksgiving, this is April," said my father.

"Maybe he forgot. And only just remembered," suggested Ma.

"Ape Face? He never forgets anything—a perfect person," I said acidly. "Anyway, why don't you ask him?"

"Yes, Ellen, why don't you? After all, twelve cans of soup don't just vanish into thin air."

"Eleven," I said tartly.

"Eleven," he conceded.

"Stop it, you two," said my mother. She went to the door of the room and yelled for Ape Face.

"Hi Mom, hi Dad, hi Annabel. Did you want me?"

"Ben," said my father. "This morning, did you, by any wild chance, take some cans of soup to school?"

"To school? No!" He sounded shocked.

"Did you," said Dad, drumming his fingers on my desk, "take eleven cans of soup, period?"

"Yes, but I didn't take them to school."

"What did you do with them?"

Ape Face looked distinctly uneasy. "Um," he said.

"That is not very informative," said Dad sternly. "Stop staring at your sneakers and give me a straight answer. *What did you do with them?*"

"I forget."

"You FORGET?!" Dad looked over at me. I shook my head. "I am told you never forget. Now, one more time: What . . . did . . . you . . ."

"Okay, okay," Ape Face said wearily. "I threw them away. In the outside garbage."

"You did *what*?!" said my parents in unison.

"Threw them away. So we wouldn't get sick."

"That's the most deranged thing I ever heard. Soup doesn't make you sick; soup is *good* for you," said Dad.

"Soup is especially good for you if you *are* sick, and now you've thrown mine out. Thanks a lump," I said, glaring at him.

He glared right back. "If you'd of eaten *that* soup you would of gotten dead."

"It just so happens I did eat some of that soup."

"You did?" said Ape Face in a shocked whisper.

"Yes, I did. And as you can see, I'm not a bit dead."

"Not yet. But soon maybe. That soup had a disease. A very bad disease."

"Oh yeah? Like what?"

"It's called botch . . . uh, botch, botchulum!" he finished triumphantly. "It kills you. Mom, if Annabel dies, can I move into her room? It's bigger than mine."

That shut us all up for a minute. Then Ma said, "Ben, darling, come here to me, will you?" She put out her arms and he slipped in. Brushing the hair off his face, she said gently, "Annabel is not going to die. All she has is a bad cold, so don't be afraid. As for what you call botchulum, the word is botulism. Botulism is extremely rare—canning companies are very, very careful about that. I don't think you need worry about it. Whatever put it into your head in the first place?"

"I dunno," said the Ape vaguely.

"It isn't as though the cans were dented or rusty or bulging."

"No . . . but . . ."

"But what?" prompted my father.

"Oh, nothing." Now, he was being not just vague but downright evasive. I can always tell. As they say, it takes one to know one.

"From where I sit, chucking out perfectly good cans of food is not nothing. There is no room in the budget for extravagant whims. Kindly bear that in mind, Sport, okay?"

"Okay," muttered the Ape, and fled from the room.

"The kid's a lunatic," said Dad.

"I think he must be going through some kind of hypochondriacal phase. Or else he's afraid of death. I'll look it up in Spock," said my mother. I pronounced him just plain malicious. Ma accused me of being uncharitable, but when I pointed out it was my dinner he'd chucked out, not theirs, she relented and brought me Jell-O instead.

Friday, April 19

THE NEXT DAY, Ma went back to school and I spent the morning watching game shows and soap operas. By midafternoon, I was so lonely even Ape Face was a welcome sight; so although he's not supposed to watch television (except for the aforementioned *Sesame Street, The Electric Company,* and *Mister Rogers*), I invited him in to see *Women's Prison* on Channel 9. He said *Abbott and Costello* was terrifically funny—why didn't we watch that? After a morning of soppy junk like John Loves Mary But Mary Loves Paul's Illegitimate Son, a little comic relief didn't sound like a bad idea, and at four o'clock we tuned in *Abbott and Costello* on Channel 11.

Okay, folks, are you ready for this? I wasn't:

At four ten, *Abbott and Costello* disappeared from the screen and a newscaster came on.

"We interrupt this program to bring you an important bulletin. Two cases of botulism have been reported in the Metropolitan area. . . ."

"See?!" exclaimed Ape Face vengefully.

"Shut up, I want to hear." I had a nasty pain in my stomach, suddenly.

". . . One victim, Charles Polistes of 320 East 73rd Street, Manhattan, is said to be in critical condition in New York Hospital; and the other, Mrs. Margaret Murphy of Dogwood Lane, Rye, is near death in the United Hospital in Port Chester. Both Polistes and Mrs. Murphy had apparently been drinking Aunt Ethel's Quik 'n Easy Sorrel Soup. . . ."

"See, see?! I told you," said Ape Face.

"*I* told *you* to shut up," I said, feeling sicker by the minute.

". . . Botulism is an extremely serious, frequently fatal disease. Symptoms of fatigue, dizziness, and shortness of breath generally occur within eighteen hours of ingesting the botulinus organism, and death usually occurs within eighteen to thirty-six hours." Thank God! It had been way over thirty-six hours since I'd ingested anything but Jell-O. My stomach felt better.

The announcement continued. "An investigation of the Aunt Ethel's Quik 'n Easy plant in Bayonne, New Jersey, is being conducted, and grocery-store managers have been alerted to remove all Aunt Ethel's Quik 'n Easy products from their shelves; but private citizens are urged to check their own shelves. We repeat: Check your shelves for Aunt Ethel's Quik 'n

Easy products. They may be extremely dangerous."

Abbott and Costello reappeared.

"Turn it off," I commanded.

"Can't I wait 'til the part with the pecan pie?"

"I said TURN IT OFF!" I thundered, making a lunge at the controls. Ape hastily turned it off.

"Now," I said. "There are a couple of things I want to ask."

"Aren't you going to thank me for trying to save your life?"

"Thanks. Now in the first place . . ."

"You're welcome."

"Don't interrupt. Listen. About this botulism business. How did you know about it yesterday when nobody else did? And why didn't you tell us you knew and warn us, instead of just throwing the cans out and then when Ma and Dad asked you what you did with them, you just stood there like a jerk going buh-duh, buh-duh?"

"I didn't!"

"Yes, you did!"

"First I said buh-duh, buh-duh, but then I told them about the botchulum."

"Botul*ism.* Yes, but how did you *know?*"

"Uh . . ."

"Don't interrupt, I'm not finished. What about that snowstorm. If it took New York, New Jersey, and Connecticut, not to mention me, by surprise, how come it didn't take you by surprise? What are you anyway—a midget clairvoyant? Where do you get your advance info from—God?"

"Television."

"You're lying." At the time, God seemed infinitely more plausible.

"Ben, do you think I'm a complete moron? That news about Aunt Ethel's Quik 'n Easy came over the air only five minutes ago. It was an emergency bulletin or they wouldn't have broken in on a program for it. It must have just happened because I've been watching for hours and there hasn't been a word about it. Besides, you've been in school all morning, nowhere near a television set, so when could you have heard it on television?"

"Yesterday I heard it!"

"Impossible! I keep telling you that's impossible. It only just happened."

Ape Face was unshakable. "I know it *sounds* weird," he began.

At last I was getting somewhere. "To put it mildly. So what's the real story?"

"That is the real story. Honestly. Yesterday afternoon I was watching *Abbott and Costello* and then the man said about the soup. I didn't want to tell Mom and Dad where I heard it because I'm not supposed to watch TV."

"What set were you watching, pray tell? The Sony was in here all day yesterday and the big set is out being fixed." Now I had him!

"Promise you won't rat?"

I nodded.

"I was watching mine."

"You mean that wrecked-up thing you bought from Boris?"

"It's not wrecked up anymore," he said proudly. "I fixed it. I fiddled around and fiddled around and then last Thursday I finally got it working great."

"That's unbelievable!"

"No, it's not. I'm good at fixing things."

"Ape Face, you're missing the point entirely. Getting the set to work isn't unbelievable—knowing you, anyway—but that it shows tomorrow's programs *is*! Don't you see that? It's like predicting the future. If what you say is true, that set has been predicting the *future.* Doesn't that sound odd to you? Odd, freaky, peculiar, scary, or anything?"

"It sounds like I didn't fix it quite right." Aargh! How could a person be so dense!

Ape Face continued, "I guess it doesn't matter, really. I don't care what day I watch a show on anyway. I mean a *Roadrunner* cartoon that's supposed to be on Wednesday is just as good on Tuesday. As long as the set works, that's all I care about. And it works."

In a pig's eye! Determined to put an end to this once and for all, I leaped out of bed and climbed into my bathrobe.

"Show me," I demanded.

"Not unless you swear not to tell Mom. Do you?"

"I swear."

"Swear on the Bible."

"Find me a Bible."

"I don't know where one is."

"Neither do I." He folded his arms and waited. Stubborn little you-know-what.

"If I cross my heart and hope to die, would you buy that instead?"

"I guess so," he said reluctantly. "Lemme see you do it." I did it. What difference could it make? The kid was off his rocker anyway.

"Okay, now show me. Wait a sec—where's the *TV Guide*? I know it's around here someplace. I was using it this morning."

"What do you need it for?"

"So I can check out what's supposed to be on tomorrow and see if it's on today, dumb-dumb. Not that I believe you. Come on, help me look."

The first thing we found was the next week's issue, and then we finally located the current one: behind the bed, under a pile of Kleenex. Grabbing the *TV Guides* in one hand and the Ape's skinny little arm in the other, I yanked him down the hall to his room.

"Close the door," he said. "I don't want Mattie to hear."

"Mattie's at the other end of the apartment. She can't hear anything."

"Even so," he said, and closed the door himself.

"All right. Now show me. Turn on . . . um . . ." I leafed through *TV Guide* 'til I got to Friday afternoon, four thirty. "Turn on Channel 11—*Superman.*"

"Neat-o," he said with enthusiasm—which was replaced by instant dejection as soon as the set came to life.

"Aw, shoot, I forgot! That's not *Superman*—that's *I Love Lucy.* Who wants to see that?" With shaking fingers, I turned to the other issue: Saturday afternoon, four thirty, Channel 11. *I Love Lucy.* Who wants to see that is right!

"Ape Face, switch channels. Try 4."

". . . brings you the New York Mets-Cincinnati Reds Game, live from Shea Stadium."

"Great! I love the Mets, don't you?"

"Not today I don't," I said grimly, checking the *TV Guide* again. "They're not supposed to play the Reds 'til tomorrow. *The Courtship of Eddie's Father* is supposed to be on."

"Saw that yesterday," said Ape Face, completely immersed in the ball game. "It was pretty good."

Mind-boggling—absolutely mind-boggling! Even with a clear head it would have been mind-boggling, but with a head full of cold, and the thoughts inching their way like molasses from synapse to synapse, it was utterly beyond me. Pleading dizziness, I rushed to my room and beeped Boris seventeen times in a row.

"For God's sake, what's the matter with you, Annabel? I heard you the first time."

"Then why didn't you answer?"

"When you're signaling I can't transmit—remember?"

"Sorry. I forgot. Listen, Boris, can you come down?"

"Now? I'm in the middle of a current events paper. How about later?" Later wasn't soon enough to suit me.

"No, now," I insisted.

"Okay, but I can't stay long. Besides, you probably shouldn't have visitors; your cold sounds terrible."

"Oh no, it's much better," I assured him.

"Then why is your voice so hoarse?"

"Fear. Sheer animal terror."

"I'll be right there," he said promptly.

"Come down the back stairs and I'll let you in the kitchen door," I croaked.

"Right," he said.

By the time I got to the kitchen, he was already buzzing the back door.

"Are there more than one?" he asked.

"More than one what?"

"Burglars."

I stared at him blankly. "Burglars?"

"You said you were hoarse with fear, and then you told me to come in the back way. I figured burglars. What else could it be?"

"You'd be amazed," I said drily. "Anyway, it's not burglars."

"Then what did you get me down here for? I told you I was in the middle of a current events paper."

"Stick around 'til the six o'clock news and I might be able to be of service to you. Follow me."

Ape Face jumped up guiltily when we came in, and then, seeing it was only us, sat back down.

"Hiya, Boris. Look! I got your set to work."

"Good for you. I didn't think it could be done." To me, he said, "Is that what you dragged me down here for? To show me how he fixed the set? You could have told me that over the walkie-talkie."

"No, I couldn't have. You just wait."

"Hey Boris," said Ape Face. "The Mets are ahead two runs. Don't you want to watch?"

"No," said Boris crossly.

I said, "Yes you do, Boris. You most definitely do. First, read this." I pointed to the place in *TV Guide* where it said under Saturday: NY Mets–Cincinnati Reds, live, Shea Stadium.

"So?"

"So now look at the TV screen: The Mets and the Cincinnati Reds at Shea Stadium. The Mets are still playing the Montreal Expos today. Doesn't that strike you as odd?"

"So what? It's probably a rerun."

"No, it's live," said Ape Face happily.

"Tell him, Ape Face," I said. "Start at the beginning and tell him the whole thing."

Just then the phone rang. Mattie can't write messages down without her reading glasses so I ran to answer it. It was my mother. How was I? Fine. Cold better? Much. Ben? He was fine, too. Anybody call? No. Was everything all right? After a second's hesitation—yes. Did I feel well enough to feed Ben and put him to bed if she went directly from Columbia to the Brasserie to have dinner with Daddy? Sure. Three minutes' worth of small talk to relieve her sense of guilt over not coming home to her chickies, then a lengthy farewell with Take-care's and I-love-you's, then Good-bye—good-bye.

When I returned, Ape Face was again looking at the ball game and Boris was looking speculatively off into space.

"Close the door," said Ape Face. A regular paranoia doll: Wind it up and it says "Close the door."

"Mattie's not around and Ma isn't coming home 'til after dinner. You can relax."

"Oh. Good. Could I see *TV Guide*?" I handed it to him.

"Boris, did he tell you?"

"Yes. Yes, he did," said Boris slowly.

"Well, what do you think? Don't you think it's spooky? Doesn't it just blow your mind?"

"Kind of," admitted Boris. "But I don't know what you were so frightened of."

"Spooky things frighten me. Ever since last year when I turned into . . ."

"Let's not go into *that* again," said Boris abruptly. (He never did believe me.) "This is different. This I can see with my own eyes. And this has some quite interesting possibilities. Listen, if it's okay with you, I think I'll take you up on your invitation to stick around for the six o'clock news."

Ape Face looked up from *TV Guide*. "Unh-unh," he said. "*The Mask of Dimitrios* is on at six."

"Why don't you watch it on the other set, tomorrow?" suggested Boris. "You'll see the same picture."

"Tomorrow's no good. Mom'll be home and she won't let me. Why don't you watch the news on the other set?"

"Because that's *not* the same. If I want to watch today's news, I can go back upstairs. I'd like to see tomorrow's news."

"Well, I wouldn't," said Ape Face flatly, "and it's my set. You sold it to me for fifty cents."

"Which you never paid me, right?"

"Ape Face!" I said, shocked to the core. "Is that true?"

"I haven't got it saved up yet, but I'm going to," he said desperately.

"Listen, squirt," said Boris, "when you buy something from a company on time—a stove, let's say—and you renege on the payments, the company repossesses your stove."

"TAKE THE STOVE!" shrieked Ape Face. "I hate eating anyway!"

"Hey, fellas, cool it, will you?" I said. "There's got to be a way to settle this." Ape Face put his hand on my arm. In a tone that would melt the heart of Hitler, he said, "Annabel, will you lend me fifty cents?"

"If you do," warned Boris, "I'll bust my half of the walkie-talkie and you'll never hear from me again."

"That is scummy emotional blackmail!"

"Call it what you will," said Boris defiantly.

"You mean to tell me you'd destroy our friendship for the sake of some dumb television set?"

Boris shrugged. "Annabel, I hope it doesn't come to that. But it's entirely up to you," he said. "Of course, if your brother wants to return what's rightfully mine . . ." His unfinished sentence hung in the air like a guillotine.

"But I don't want to," said Ape Face, his eyes filling up with tears.

"All right, Ape Face, turn off the waterworks and listen to me for a minute. Here's what *I* think: *I* think Boris is being extremely unreasonable and I don't know why that set is so important to him; but if he insists on having it back, you should return it to him."

"Aw, Annabel," moaned Ape Face, stabbed to the quick.

I shot him a pipe-down-I-have-it-all-under-control-look, and continued.

"Wait a minute, I haven't finished. I think you should return it to him—*in the exact condition in which you received it.*"

"You mean wrecked up?"

"Exactly. Where's your screwdriver?"

Boris was horrified. "You *wouldn't*!" he said in a strangled whisper.

"Oh, wouldn't I?" I said casually, as I rummaged around in the Ape's toolbox. "After all, Boris, you want to play legal eagle, look at it this way: Your stove company has the right to repossess the original merchandise, but a miracle stove that cooks tomorrow night's dinner? They have to pay more for that—let's say three hundred dollars which I happen to know you don't have. So . . ." I produced the screwdriver, and with a flourish handed it to Ape Face. "Go to it, kid."

"Okay, F. Lee Bailey," Boris said in a very ungracious tone. "You win. But with your kind permission, I'd like to ask your client a couple of questions."

"Certainly," I said. I instructed my client to turn off the ball game, which had just finished anyway, and pay attention.

"Now tell me," said Boris, "what do you watch on television?"

"*Huckleberry Hound, The Beverly Hillbillies, The Match Game, Nanny and the Professor,* movies—"

"In other words, taped stuff or reruns, right?"

"Guess so," said Ape Face.

"No live stuff?" Boris was moving in for the kill. I could sense it, although I didn't know what he had in mind. Neither did Ape Face, who wanted to know what was "live stuff."

"News. Up-to-the-minute news—that's live stuff. You like that?"

"No," said Ape Face. "It's boring. Dead stuff is better—like *The Mask of Dimitrios,*" he added balefully. "What time is it now? I don't want to miss it."

"Only ten of six. Don't worry." Ape Face looked dubious. Boris squatted down on his haunches so he was face-to-face with him.

"Listen, pal, I'm about to make you a terrific deal. I'll swap you this old pile of junk for my brand-new Motorola. You can watch all the dead stuff you want from morning to night in glorious living color instead of grainy black and white. How about it?"

Ape Face thought for a second. "Will I still owe you the fifty cents?"

"Naah," said Boris magnanimously. "What's a little debt like that between friends? Do we have a deal?"

Ape Face thought for another second. Then he

frowned and heaved a deep sigh. Uh-oh, I thought. Here it comes.

"I'm sorry," he said. Boris collapsed on the floor in dismay.

"What do you mean, sorry?"

"I think he means no," I said. Boris glared at me.

"Who asked you? This is between me and your client. When he wants advice from counsel he'll ask for it. Now listen, pal, what do you mean, sorry? How could you pass up a terrific deal like that; are you stupid or something? Give me one good reason."

"The reason is because when my mother is home and I want to watch television, all I have to do is just close the door and play 'Yellow Submarine' loud on the record player so she won't hear anything. She never comes in without knocking because I have this 'Don't come in without knocking first' sign on the door. When she knocks, I turn the set off fast."

"So why can't you play 'Yellow Submarine' and watch my color Motorola just as well?"

"I could. But what would happen when I was at school and she came in to put my socks away or some-thing and saw a brand-new set? The old set she doesn't think works, so I'd rather keep it."

"If counsel could be permitted to make a suggestion," I began.

"My pleasure," said Boris sarcastically. "But it better be good. And it better be acceptable to both parties."

"Well," I said. "To begin with, I'm sure my client is most grateful for your kind offer of a Motorola color TV and regrets not being able to accept it; don't you, Ape?" Ape Face obediently manufactured a toothy smile of appreciation.

"What would he accept? My head on a platter, I suppose."

"Yich!" said Ape Face, turning away in disgust.

"My client is too young to understand literary or biblical references," I announced. "May I continue?"

Boris nodded curtly.

"Counsel would like to suggest that although a twenty-one inch Motorola would not be acceptable, my client might feel differently about one of those teensy-weensy battery-powered Sonys—small enough to be concealed in a toy chest underneath the Lego where the mother of the client never looks."

"Oh man, *I'd* like one of those, too!" said Ape Face enthusiastically.

"Evidently, your client is also too young to understand legal jargon."

"Yes, I don't," agreed Ape Face cheerfully.

"Okay, in plain English, Boris wants to know if you'd be satisfied with a teensy-weensy Sony? The latest model, of course." Nothing ventured, nothing gained.

"Boris also wants to know," said Boris, quivering with rage, "where Boris is going to lay his mitts on such an expensive item when he just blew his last remaining bucks on a birthday present for counsel!"

"I know where," said Ape Face. "The store where you got the Motorola. You take the set in there—tomorrow, maybe—and say to the store man, 'I'm about to make you a terrific deal. I'll swap you one of those dinky little Sonys for this brand-new Motorola I just bought from you. How about it?' He'll be glad to do it because a big set is better than a small set. Then, when you bring me the Sony, I'll be glad to swap you back your old pile of junk. Do we have a deal?"

Frankly, I was beginning to feel like a vestigial organ. I mean, what does a con artist need with a lawyer?

"So how about it, Boris. Do we have a deal or don't we?" Ape Face said again.

"I guess so," said Boris, "but on a contingency basis."

Even I didn't know what that meant. "Plain English, please. My client . . ."

"Your client is a pain in the neck! Your client has a deal contingent on my being able to watch the six o'clock news, *right here*, on *this set*, in precisely one minute."

"Annabel, can I take back my deal?"

"Let me think about that," I said.

Boris jumped up and switched on the set. "There is no time to think about that. I've had it to the eyeballs with both of you. If Ape Face is so damn determined to see that stupid-jerk movie, he is cordially invited to come to my house tomorrow at six o'clock and watch it there on my mother's set. He can even stay for dinner if he wants to."

"Me, too?" I wanted to know.

"Of course, you, too. You think I want to baby-sit that creep Shylock by myself?"

"Boris, I'm flabbergasted! You mean I'm finally going to get to see your house?"

"For what it's worth, yes."

"And meet your mother?" A staggering development! I could hardly believe my ears.

"She won't be there. She has a date or something." Nuts!

"Who's going to make dinner for us?" Ape Face asked. "Are you, Boris? Because if it's you, maybe I'll just stay for the movie." (Boris's cooking, which Ape Face and I had occasion to sample last year, is highly imaginative but a trifle exotic for a seven-year-old palate.)

"It just so happens the maid is coming tomorrow. She'll cook dinner. Will that suit Your Highness?"

"Sure," said Ape Face cheerfully. "I think I'll go ride my bike in the hall. You want to shake on the deal, first?"

"If I shook your hand now, I'd probably crunch it to bits," growled Boris, without lifting his eyes from the television screen. "Everybody shut up. Here comes the six o'clock news."

"Out, out!" I whispered to Ape Face. "I'll take care of your deal. As counsel, I'm empowered."

So for a solid hour, we watched the news to find out what goodies were going to go on in the world tomorrow. Boris, scribbling furiously in a lined composition book he found in the bookshelf, took voluminous notes on the U.S.–Russian grain deal, a Turkish military coup, the hijacking of a Japanese 747, a detailed report on the botulism bit (since the bulletin I'd seen, the man had died but the woman was still hanging in there), a rave review for a movie that opened at the Paris theater, the Mets–Cincinnati Reds game ("a triumph for Cincinnati and a sad Saturday for the home team"), the weather ("after yesterday's downpour, New Yorkers basked in sixty-two-degree sunshine. An estimated ten thousand people gathered in Sheep Meadow to fly kites, and bike paths were jammed"), and a couple of Metropolitan horror stories. ("The decapitated body of an unidentified male was discovered lodged behind the pins in a Bronx bowling alley, and a three-alarm flash fire gutted the Lullabye Lingerie factory at 43 Bleecker Street at four o'clock this afternoon. No lives were lost, although the watchman who was rescued from the fourth floor of the building told Chief Inspector Mullin that had the fire occurred on a weekday rather than today, thirty-seven employees might have perished in the inferno.") Finally, when the paper towel commercial began, I turned off the set.

"Well, what do you think?" I asked.

"Sh, I'm thinking," said Boris. For several minutes, he sat totally immersed in his notes, one hand absent-mindedly tugging at a hunk of his chestnut hair and the other twiddling a pencil between his upper and lower teeth. *Clickety-clickety-clickety.* Loathsome sound!

"Must you?" I complained.

"Must I what? Oh . . . sorry," he said, wiping the pencil off on his pants. "I forget I'm doing it."

"I know. You always do it when you're thinking. So what *are* you thinking?"

"I am thinking that this thing," he nodded toward the set, "is so incredible, I don't know *what* to think. It's supernatural. It can't happen, *how* can it happen?"

"Maybe it's like ESP. At Barron University they have lots of data on people who are clairvoyant."

"People maybe, but a *television* set?"

"No, I suppose not. Anyway, what's the good of wondering how it happened, Boris? The fact is, it did. Actually, it's going to come in quite handy. Take weather predictions, for instance. Half the time they stink. From now on, you'll be able to beep me on the beeper and say things like, 'There was a hailstorm tomorrow—wear boots.' Like that freak blizzard the

Ape kept trying to tell me . . . What's the matter? Why do you have that terrible, supercilious sneer on your face?"

"Because I am stupefied by your total lack of imagination. Annabel, don't you realize that all this stuff I've written down—we are the only two people alive who know about it? And that that pile of junk we've been looking at has got to be the most extraordinary collection of atoms and molecules ever assembled by man or God?! Don't you understand the potential of a thing like this? To have a twenty-four-hour jump on the rest of the whole world and all you can think of to use it for is the WEATHER?!" Breathless, he brandished his notes under my nose and managed to cough out two final words of insult: "Earthbound idiot!"

"Listen, wise guy—" Sometimes Boris can be insufferable, "—if *you* were the one who could've not gotten a foul case of flu if only you hadn't not known about a big snowstorm, you'd think about the weather, too."

"My compliments on your exquisite syntax. Would you care to repeat that sentence?"

"No, I wouldn't," I retorted. "Furthermore, since I had to sit in stony silence for five minutes while you munched on an Eberhard Faber No. 2, I was under the impression that you were the self-appointed thinker around here. You want me to think? I'll think—gimme those notes." I snatched them out of his hand and began reading. The third item on the list gave me a sudden chill.

"Boris!" I gasped. "That Japan Airlines plane! We've got to *do* something about that. Warn them or something."

"How?"

"Call them up and warn them."

"And say what? 'Hello, I want to report a hijacking'?"

"Sure."

"So then they say, 'Can you give us any further details?' and you say, 'A 747 on the eight A.M. flight out of Tokyo en route to Paris was hijacked somewhere over Tibet and forced to land in Beirut.' Right?" I checked Boris's notes.

"Right."

"So then, after a lengthy pause, Japan Airlines says, kind of suspicious, 'We have not received any reports of this incident. When did it occur?' And *you* say?"

"Tomorrow. It occurred tomorrow," I answered sheepishly.

"Exactly. And then they will hang up on you because they think you are a nut."

"But wait a minute, Boris. What if I say the 747 is *going* to be hijacked tomorrow? Then they wouldn't think I was a nut."

"No, then they would think you were part of the hijacking gang, setting them up for blackmail. And if they could trace the call, which knowing how long you stay on the phone they could probably do, they'd come straight here and arrest you."

"We could tell them about the set, and show it to them. Then they'd believe us."

"They might, but then we wouldn't have it anymore. Word would get out, and the government would find some way to requisition it; then scientists would pull it apart and destroy it; either that or it might fall into the hands of unscrupulous people who wanted to make money out of it."

"How could they do that?"

"I don't know. I haven't figured it out myself yet. All I know is, I don't think a call to Japan Airlines is going to prevent that hijacking anyway, even if they do believe you."

"All those poor scared passengers and the little babies. Shouldn't we at least try? Couldn't I just run to the drugstore and talk fast in a phone booth?"

Boris smiled me a gentle, warm smile, and said, "You're good people, Annabel. Really good people. Look—sit down here next to me for a minute, and I'll try to put it into words. But it's sort of confusing, so give me a minute to think."

I sat down on the bed. Boris, his mind a million miles away, took my hand and began tracing his way up and down my fingers.

"All right," he said, about a minute later. "Listen

carefully and see if you agree. This Thing, this miracle Box, oracle, mechanized prognosticator—whatever it is, is going to lead us into some very tricky areas. I don't know whether it has to do with metaphysics or philosophy or what, but when you're dealing with the future . . ." He broke off, snarled up in his thoughts, I guess.

"Go on."

"Well, I don't think the future can be changed. In other words, if our miracle Box shows us tomorrow's news, that news is definitely going to take place or we wouldn't be seeing it today. Because the Box does not *predict* events, it *shows* events that have actually taken place but will not come to pass until twenty-four hours later. Are you with me so far?" I nodded.

"Next point: We can't prevent events that have already happened in the future, but we can benefit from advance knowledge that they are going to."

"Like the botulism business. Or the blizzard."

"Yes. Or other things."

"Like what?"

"Well, staying home when you know there's going to be a blizzard is avoiding a bad thing. Like tomorrow I was going to ask you if you wanted to go bike riding, but the bike paths are going to be jammed so I won't."

"Thanks anyway."

"You're welcome. But what about taking advantage of a good thing? If you already knew a mammoth surprise sale of records happened at Goody's tomorrow, wouldn't you get there first thing in the morning? And if I know, on Sunday, that the Mets are going to win on Monday, I can make a bet with my friend Chuckie Waterman Monday morning in school (and win, naturally). That's taking advantage of a good thing."

"That's taking advantage of a good friend. Doesn't sound too ethical to me."

"So okay, I'll bet Harvey Kuchel instead. He's a guy I hate."

"Is taking advantage of an enemy any better? More fun, but is it any better, ethically speaking?"

"When I want a spiritual advisor, I'll ask for one," said Boris impatiently. "Besides, I was only giving you a what-if. I might not do that at all. I'm only trying to explain to you, in theory, what a gold mine we've got here"—he patted the Box lovingly—"and how we'd be fools not to put it to work for us. Tomorrow," he said, smiling in happy anticipation, "I'm going to turn in the Motorola for the Sony, and tomorrow night when you and the Ape come up to watch the movie, you can bring this little baby with you. Then I'll study the whole situation more closely and come up with some plans."

"I don't know, Boris," I said uneasily. "Maybe I won't like your plans."

"Then maybe I won't tell you about them. Don't forget, it's my set."

"Not yet it isn't. We haven't made the deal yet, remember? And we're not going to, either, unless you agree to a few conditions of mine. Fine type you are—when I'm trying to save the lives of a hundred and forty hijack victims, you say 'Oh, no, because the set might fall into the hands of unscrupulous people who want to make money out of it.' What do you call you—*scru*pulous?!"

"Yes!" he said fiercely. "Yes, I am. But I also need money. I don't want to go into it now, but believe me, Annabel, I do. So I've just got to have the Box. Are you going to make the deal or not?"

"I guess so," I muttered. "But I sure hope I'm not making a mistake."

On his way out the door, Boris hastily and heartily assured me I wasn't—and ironically enough, he turned out to be right. A mistake, after all, is a little thing. You give a cab driver a five-dollar bill instead of a one; or you dial the wrong area code and get Anchorage, Alaska. Those are what I call mistakes. Chicken-feed folly. Consummating that deal between Boris and my brother was not, therefore, what you could call a mistake—it was what you could call a catastrophic, cataclysmic boo-boo.

Saturday, April 20

THE NEXT MORNING, the botulism thing was all over the front page of the *Times.* My father read the entire piece out loud to my mother at the breakfast table, and then said, "Ben, it seems we owe you an apology and a vote of thanks." The Ape grinned through a disgusting mouthful of scrambled eggs, and I lost my appetite altogether—partly from looking at him, but mostly from dread of what was coming next. I didn't have long to wait. My mother is no dummy.

"Benjie, wasn't it Thursday you threw out those cans?" He nodded and swallowed.

"Isn't that odd, Bill? You'd almost think he knew."

"Couldn't have, it only happened yesterday," said my father. "Anyway, don't ask me, ask him." Ape Face's mouth was empty now, and I was scared to death of what might come out of it in the way of words, so I asked him if he wanted his bacon—if not, could I have it? Being a real dog-in-the-manger type, he immediately stuffed all three strips in at once.

"Tell us your secret, Benjie," said my mother, teasingly. "How did you find out? Or was it just a lucky coincidence?"

"Coincidence," I said, kicking him under the table.

"Is your name Benjie?" said my father. "Let him speak for himself."

"With his *mouth* full?! You never let me do that." At this point, Ape Face mumbled something about having to go to the bathroom, and left the room. By the time he came back, I'd managed to steer the subject of conversation around to what we were all going to do on this beautiful sunny day. Ma and Dad and Ape Face decided to go biking in the park (good luck to them!) and I decided to go window-shopping in the Village with my friend Virginia. Ma wanted to know if I'd pick up some pork chops for dinner, which reminded me to tell her that Ape Face and I had been invited to Boris's for dinner if that was all right with her. It was.

At around twelve, they all three plowed out the door, swaddled in sweaters and mufflers up to their ears, poor things, and I was poking through my closet, looking for something suitable for sixty-two degrees, when Boris beeped me.

"Just thought you'd be interested in knowing that last night, after I left you, I got really worried about that plane. In fact, I was up half the night thinking about it. So at seven this morning, *I* went to the drugstore and made a quick call to Japan Airlines."

"How terrific of you. But why didn't you call from home?"

"I told you, my mother doesn't want me to use the phone."

"Even one little call? Boy, she must be an ogre."

"No comment. Also, I didn't want to take a chance on them tracing the call. Listen, do you want to hear what happened or don't you?"

"Yes indeedy. What happened?"

"I told them their eight A.M. 747 out of Tokyo enroute to Paris was going to be hijacked."

"Did they think you were a nut? Or a gangster?"

"No," said Boris, sounding rather bemused. "They thought I was a nuisance."

"A nuisance?! Why? I don't understand. What did they say?"

"I thought you'd never ask. They said, 'We already have that information, sir.'"

"That is utterly impossible. How could they have known at seven when the plane didn't take off 'til eight?"

"Exactly what I asked them. The explanation, my dear Good Samaritan, is so simple, it's funny." He began to chortle—just to prove how funny it was, I suppose. I was not amused.

"If it's so simple, let's have it."

"The time change!" he gurgled. "The eight A.M. 747 from Tokyo to Paris took off at *six* P.M. *last night,* New York time. Japan Airlines had known about the hijacking for hours. They were very polite and patient but they said I was the sixteenth call they'd received today from concerned citizens, and under the circumstances I could surely understand how busy they were; they thanked me for my concern and hung up. . . . Are you still there?"

"Yes. I'm trying to figure it out. Just as I think I've got it straight, it eludes me again."

"I know what you mean," he said. "The point is, we didn't watch the news until six o'clock last night, but if we'd watched earlier, on our set, we probably would have gotten the news in the morning. Or maybe even late the night before. Like all those other people who called up *this* morning."

"Aw, nuts! It's a real bummer, isn't it?"

"It's what you get when you mess around with the future, Annabel. I told you last night, I don't think it can be done. Frankly, that's why I made the call—to *see* if it could be done; but fate intervened."

"You want to call it fate, go ahead. I call it stupidity. One of us should have thought of the time change."

"*Even if we had, we still didn't turn the set on early enough to do anything about it.* That was fate, wasn't it? My God, you're the most stubborn person I ever met! I was up all night thinking about your problem;

then I got up at six thirty and ran to the corner to do something about your problem; and now I have to trundle a two-ton Motorola downtown for a trade-in to solve your brother's problem—which will be a big hassle—on no sleep. I don't want to talk anymore. I'll see you at six. Roger, over, and out."

"Roger, over, and out. And drop dead!"

If I'd known what kind of mood I was going to be in, I would never have made a date with Virginia. Virginia's a person who can drive you right up the wall unless you're in a tolerant frame of mind. She never used to be like that. As recently as two years ago she was a neat kid, but now she has Theatrical Aspirations and a lot of annoying habits. Like correcting your grammar. As it happens, I have an extremely good grasp of my native tongue and grades to prove it, but I don't bother to talk the way I write. Who does? Virginia does, that's who. If you say "Everybody's finished their assignment," she says, "His and her assignment." (Our school is coed.) If you say, "I know a boy you'd get along great with," she says "A boy with whom you'd get along beautifully." If you knock on the bathroom door and say, "It's only me," she says, "It's only I" (to which you are tempted to retort, "Never mind, I didn't really want to come in, anyway"). The colloquial use of the word "like" engenders in her such scorn that most of us have dropped the word from our vocabularies altogether.

Virginia used to be a fabulous basketball player, but now she gets out of gym at the drop of a hat. The excuses are varied and wondrous: sinus headaches, migraine headaches (pronounced meegraine), raging fevers (usually pronounced nonexistent by the school nurse), low blood sugar, fatigue, and when all else fails, her monthly Excuse which, if legitimate, she employs with such alarming frequency it's a miracle she hasn't died by now.

She also tends to dress nicely for school, which is her way of putting the rest of us down, I guess, because I can't think of a single other reason why she'd bother. None of the other kids do. ("Does," according to Virginia.)

Nevertheless, I still like her. I've known her ever since we were in nursery school together. That's going back a long time. We've got memories. For instance, in the fourth grade, she wanted to be class president and she made me her secret campaign manager. I did such a good job of being nice to people, they elected me instead. When we were ten, I slept over at her house one night and we spent a delightful couple of hours burning Kleenex in the toilet. Unfortunately, we also burned the bottom of the toilet seat in the process. This didn't go over too well with Virginia's mother, who deducted a usurious percentage from both our allowances for six weeks following. Oh yes, we've got memories, all right—and scars. In a towering rage over

I-no-longer-remember-what, I once threw my Indian-beaded belt at her, and accidentally cut her forehead open with the buckle. (Two stitches for her, remorse for me.)

After all these years, we've got a certain rapport going for us; we know each other so well we can catch each other's vibes from across a room. Right now, she's going through a stage I don't particularly admire, but if I could put up with a whole year of her thinking she was a five-gaited thoroughbred mare, I guess I can put up with this. At least now she talks. It's pretty fancy dialogue, but a vast improvement over whinnies and neighs. By next year, she'll probably be out of this stage and into something else. And anyway, she's an old friend.

When I got off the number thirty bus in front of Tiffany's, where Virginia and I had agreed to meet, she was already there, waiting for me. Correction: She was not waiting for me. She was admiring a gem in the window—the gem being herself, of course. It beats me why she bothers to window-shop at all. She could save a ton of shoe leather if she just stayed home all day in front of a full-length mirror.

"Hey, how's things?" I said.

"Hallo, luv," said Virginia. Who does she think she is today, I speculated—some English movie star?

She leaned over to give me a cool kiss on the cheek. I backed off.

"What's new?" I inquired.

"Not a bloody thing," she sighed. "Except, look at this, will you?" She sucked in her breath and patted her tiny tummy. "Bloat. Sheer bloat. It's *too* depressing!"

"You want to see bloat, get a load of this," I said, pulling up my turtleneck to display my own gorgeous gut. "If I get any fatter, I'm going to have an outsie belly button."

"Navel," gently chided Virginia. "If it bothers you so much, why don't you try some abdominal exercises?"

"It doesn't bother me *that* much," I said, yanking down my sweater before I was arrested for indecent exposure.

"It's up to you, darling girl," said Virginia blandly, "but if I were you, I'd keep an eye. What size are you?"

"Ten," I said defiantly.

"Are you *really*? In what—a caftan?"

That made me so mad I refused to talk to her all the way downtown on the Fifth Avenue bus. For forty-eight solid blocks, I sang "Parsley, Sage, Rosemary and Thyme" over and over again while Virginia pretended it wasn't driving her crazy.

By the time we had scrutinized both sides of Christopher Street, it was driving *me* crazy, so I switched to "I Don't Know How to Love Him" from *Jesus Christ Superstar,* and Virginia counterattacked with "Row, Row, Row Your Boat." People were now beginning to look at us as though we were demented, which, considering what passes for normal in that neighborhood, should give you some idea of what we must have looked and sounded like.

Finally, in a hamburger joint on Greenwich Avenue, a détente was reached in the following manner.

Virginia said, "I'm positively famished, aren't you?"

I said, "Yeah."

"What are you going to eat?"

"A bacon cheeseburger with onion rings and French fries on the side. And a chocolate shake," I said, fixing her with a steely stare. "And you?"

"A lemon Tab," said Virginia with a martyred smile. Diet one-upmanship!

"I thought you were so famished."

"I am, but I'm taking you to lunch and I don't want to run out of money."

"In that case, *I'll* have the lemon Tab," I said politely.

"Oh no, please," she protested. "It's my treat. I want you to have whatever you want."

"I want a lemon Tab."

"Right you are. I think I'll have the bacon cheeseburger with onion rings and French fries on the side. Plus a vanilla shake. Plus a jelly doughnut," said Virginia, and the fight was over. Not because she paid for my lunch but because she allowed me the satisfaction of watching her gorge herself while I abstained. For a weight-watcher, this is the most generous gesture you can make.

For the next two hours, we thoroughly investigated practically every shop in the Village: handmade sandals, health food, reconditioned blue jeans, second-hand books, Navajo jewelry, Appalachian Mountain quilts—the works. Virginia, exercising exemplary self-control over her tendency to be a pretentious pain, managed to get on my nerves only once: After trying on a Mexican wedding dress—which she had no intention of buying, naturally—she said to the saleswoman, "I'm awfully afraid it's no go. My brahzeeaire would show through this transparent material."

Number one: The Mexican wedding dress was made of canvas tough enough to bury a man at sea in; you couldn't see through it with a fluoroscope.

Number two: Most people call it bra, some people call it a brazeer, but nobody (except my grandmother) calls it a brahzeeaire.

Number three: Virginia has a tiny top to match her tiny tummy. She never wears a bra at all.

Anyway, by a quarter to four, we'd covered everything but the newsstands, and in passing one of those, a headline about the hijacking caught my eye. I was suddenly reminded of something.

"Hey, Virginia, where's Bleecker Street, do you know?"

"Right over there, I believe. What's on Bleecker Street?"

"Let's go see."

"Right you are," said Virginia amiably.

I steered her past a row of quaint brownstones and a few nothing shops, coming to a halt in front of Number Forty-Three: Lullabye Lingerie, Inc. I sniffed the air carefully; no smell of smoke. Starting at the roof, I scanned the building from top to bottom, and then checked the alleys on both sides; no sign of smoke either.

"What are you *doing*?" asked Virginia.

"Admiring the architecture."

"What architecture? It's a perfectly ordinary, ugly, four-story building. It's boring. Come on, let's get a move on, shall we?"

"Virginia, I spent an hour and a half watching you climb in and out of stuff you weren't even planning to buy. The least you can do is give me—" I looked at my watch; it was five to four "—five minutes. What's boring to you isn't necessarily boring to me."

"You can say that again," she said grumpily.

"If you're still bored five minutes from now, we'll go," I promised.

Resigned, Virginia crossed the street and plunked herself down on someone's front stoop.

I simply couldn't fathom it. This time, there was no time change to contend with. Four P.M. uptown is four

P.M. downtown. How could there be an inferno at four if there wasn't even a wisp of smoke now? Had I gotten mixed up on the address and this was the wrong building? Then I remembered about the watchman. If it was the right building, there was a watchman who'd been rescued from the fourth floor. Maybe he'd been asleep up there and that's how the fire got started. If so, maybe I could prevent the fire by waking him up in time. Boris's metaphysical theories notwithstanding, I felt it was my humanitarian duty to try.

I rang the bell, loud, five times.

Ah-ha! A window opened on the top floor and a hard-hat head came out.

"Whaddya want."

"I want to buy a nightie."

"So whaddya bothering a guy now for? It's Satiddy. We're closed. Buyaself a nightie somewheres else. Crazy kid!" With that, he hurled an empty beer can and an obscene epithet at me. Stepping into the street for a better aim, I accurately and loudly returned them both.

It was perfect timing. The beer can had no sooner disappeared in the window than the six o'clock news came true. A good thing I was already in the street; if I hadn't been, I would have been blasted into it by a ferocious explosion.

"Holy crumb!" screamed Virginia. "What did you do?!"

"Are you still bored?" I shouted, over the roar of the flames and the already clanging fire engines. "Stick with me, kid, it's a laugh a minute! Beats Mexican wedding dresses any day!"

I joined her on the opposite side of the street—to get a better view and to get out of the way of the engines. Within minutes, all of the East Village had joined us, including a CBS camera crew and several reporters scribbling away. The fire chief was barking instructions over a loudspeaker, and I heard him say there was probably no one in the building but they'd better check anyway.

"You bet your boots they better," I remarked to the man next to me. "There's a watchman up there on the fourth floor."

"Is that so," said the man. Without bothering to look at me, he said "How do you know?"

"She was havin' a altercation widda guy whenda buildin' blew. Kid's gotta mout' onna like a sewa!" said a pimply-faced voice to my left. I ignored it, and so did the man. We were both watching the fireman who'd been assigned to the rescue operation. He climbed in the fourth-story window and immediately climbed out again, followed by my dear friend and epithet hurler, who was greeted by an enthusiastic cheer from the crowd. I, myself, felt like booing. Not that I'd want to see him fry or anything, but he certainly wasn't a cause for celebration.

Some lady behind me was speculating about whether there was anybody else in there. I told her there wasn't, but it was a good thing it was Saturday; if it had been a weekday, thirty-seven people might have been in a lot of hot water, ha ha.

Now, the man next to me turned around and gave me a searching look.

"Just a joke," I said lamely. "I have a sick sense of humor. Black comedy, you might call it."

"You might. And then again, you might not. Tell me—you said thirty-seven people work there. How do you know that?" I was beginning to get a queasy feeling that maybe this man was more than just an interested bystander. I decided to play it dumb and casual.

"I don't *actually* know. It was a calculated guess—based on the size of the building and so forth. I mean, it wouldn't have to be thirty-seven—could be fifty, fifty-two . . . what do *you* think?" I asked.

"I think you know more than you're telling, young lady," said the man as he flashed his wallet under my nose. Detective Horgan. How do you like that? Two hundred people standing on the street, a hundred and ninety-nine of them innocent bystanders, and I strike up a conversation with a plainclothes cop!

"Yaah, yaah, baby doll, tell the nice policeman what you trun inna winda!" said the pimply-faced voice. (A hundred and ninety-*eight* interested bystanders, one cop, and one sadist.)

"Wait a *min*ute!" I began, but Pimples was grooving on the whole scene now. There was no stopping him.

"Don't tell me you didn't trun nuttin' inna winda. I sore it. Prolly a bomb!"

"Both of you, come with me, please," said Detective Horgan. Protesting feebly, I was led, followed by the witness for the prosecution, to a cluster of uniformed fire officials and policemen who were conferring in the middle of the street.

"Chief," said Detective Horgan, "I think we got a live one here. And a witness, too."

"She trun a bomb inna winda," said Dan Diction. All the guys were staring at me.

"I did *not* trun a . . ." I took a deep breath and began again, enunciating carefully and clearly, and pausing between each and every word.

"I did not throw a bomb in the window. I threw a beer can. I was, in point of fact, returning the beer can to its rightful owner who had thrown it at *me*. Ask him yourself."

"We will. Mike, go get the guy and bring him over here."

"Now," said Detective Horgan, taking out a pencil and pad. "What's your name?"

"I'm not telling you. I didn't do anything wrong so I'm not telling you. I'm pleading the—um—Fifth. And the—uh Second, the Third, and the Fourth."

Better to be safe than sorry, I always say.

"What about the First?" asked Detective Horgan.

"I'll take it," I said promptly. They all burst out laughing.

"Come on, kid. We got rights, too, you know, and one of them is you gotta tell us your name."

"Marvin the Torch," I snapped. This broke them up in a million little pieces which was all right with me. I loathe being laughed at, but being treated like a stand-up comic was better than being treated like a pyromaniac.

Mike showed up with the watchman. For someone who'd just emerged unscathed from a three-alarm fire, he was looking pretty good. Filthy but good. (He was probably filthy before the fire.)

"Chief, this is Mr.—?"

"Nickolik. Stanislaus Nickolik," said the watchman, ceremoniously shaking hands with everybody, including Detective Horgan, who immediately reached for a handkerchief and wiped himself off.

"Mr. Nickolik, meet Marvin the Torch," said the Chief with a grin.

"I already met Marva. You all right, kid? That was some blast, wasn't that some blast, huh, kid?" He threw a playful punch at me, which unfortunately landed with a grungy stain on my denim jacket.

"We were wondering if you could tell us about that," said Detective Horgan. "This gentleman here"—he indicated Pimples—"claims . . ."

"She trun a bomb!"

"A bomb?" Nickolik, who was beginning to worm his way into my heart, expressed great surprise. "—, —! She din't trow no bomb. She trew a beer can. To tell you the trute," he admitted, "she was trowin' it back after I trew it at her. Just a friendly little squabble, no harm done, right Marva?" He put his arm around me and gave me an affectionate squeeze. We were practically engaged.

"I wouldn't exactly call that no harm done," said Detective Horgan, nodding his head at the smoking ruins.

Nickolik was outraged. "She din't have nuttin' to do widdat! Inna first place, if she'd of trown a bomb into the fourt' floor, and I was on the fourt' floor which I was, you know where I'd be now? All over the fourt' floor—like raspberry jam. You could scoop me up with a spoon. And in the second place, I'll lay you five to one it was the furnace blew up."

"Oh?" said Horgan.

"Yeah. I been telling the boss and telling the boss—you don't get that furnace fixed, one of these days there's gonna be some conflagration. Confraglation. Anyway—some fire."

"Ah," they all murmured knowingly. Horgan chucked me under the chin. He should just try that again; I'll bite his finger off!

"Okay if I go now? I'm late for home," I said.

"Sure, sweetheart, run along," said Horgan. "Sorry if I caused you any inconvenience. Just trying to do my job."

"Abso*lut*ely," I said, jaunty-jolly with relief. "Chief, guys, nice meeting you." I gave an enthusiastic salute, turned on my heel, and beat a hasty retreat down the block toward Broadway.

Halfway there, I realized someone was following me.

Detective Horgan with another nosy question? A mugger? I ran faster. The person following me ran faster, too. I took a quick look over my shoulder: It was a carrot-haired man in a raincoat—clearly not Detective Horgan, but quite possibly a mugger. These days, anybody could be a mugger.

"Hey, Marvin! Marvin the Torch!" shouted the carrot-haired man.

"Leave me alone," I shouted breathlessly.

Long-distance running is not my forte. In a second, he'd caught up with me.

"Wait up!" he said, huffing and chuffing at my side. "I'm not going to hurt you—I only want to ask a couple of questions."

"I don't want to wait up. I'm late, I've got to get home, and I've answered enough questions for one day. Besides, I don't know you."

By now I was so exhausted I was reduced to a slow trot.

"Who are you anyway?"

"I'm a reporter. *Daily News,*" he panted. "Do you want to see my card?"

I came to a full stop. "Not especially." Undaunted, he whipped out his notebook.

"Just a couple of quick questions? Detective Horgan said you were a witness to the explosion. Is that right?"

"That's right."

"Could you describe it for me?"

"A big bang," I said impatiently.

"Before the explosion occurred, did you notice anything unusual, anything that might lead you to believe the explosion was not accidental?"

"Why would anyone want to blow up a nightgown factory?"

"A nightgown factory could be a front for something else. Remember that house that blew up on Eleventh Street a few years ago? The Weathermen did it. Did you notice any suspicious-looking people on the block before the explosion?"

"No. The street was completely deserted."

"Then what were you doing there?"

"Trying to buy a nightie," I snapped. "Listen, you said quick questions. I'm in a hurry."

"Just one more—would you mind telling me your real name?"

"Ann Smith." I don't think it fooled him for a

minute, but he wrote it down anyway. I also gave him a fake address and a fake age—eighteen.

"Well, Ann," he said pleasantly, "thank you for your time. I appreciate it." I thought this was quite forbearing of him, considering how unhelpful I'd been.

"You're welcome. Sorry I couldn't be of more use." He grinned at me. I noticed he had beautiful teeth and a cute nose and nice green eyes.

"I'm sure you did the best you could. But listen, if anything else does occur to you, I wish you'd call me. Here's my card—just in case."

I looked at it: Bartholomew Bacon, *Daily News,* 555-0176, ext. 421.

"Okay, Bartholomew. 'Bye now."

" 'Bye, *Ann,*" he said with a knowing wink. I winked back and dashed down the subway steps.

Saturday, April 20, later

When I got home, I found a note from Ape Face Scotch-taped to the outside of the front door:

> Dere Annabel, we had a awful time bikeing. it was to hot and my training weels fell of. Dad got all most run over by a millyun poepul trying to fix them and then he got mad so we came home soon. They are takeing a nap. *sh.* Bariss called. He said he got delaid downtown but we should go upstairs anyway the maid would let us in. He said I could watch my movie in the den. if your not here befour 6, Im going alone.
>
> LOVE
>
> Ape Face.
>
> PS you're frend called. she says to tell you your some frend. she is mad to.

What friend? Oh my God, Virginia! I completely forgot poor Virginia. Come to think of it, what do I mean "poor Virginia"? Where was she when I needed her? She could have come forth as a credible character witness, but instead she melts away—into an air-conditioned cab, no doubt—and abandons me to the hostile horde. Nuts to you, Virginia; some friend yourself!

In a rage, I crunched up the Ape's note, plunged into the dimly lit apartment—and immediately collided with a large lumpy something which was blocking my way. Whatever it was fell to the floor with a crash, and then I heard a stifled scream of anguish from my brother.

"I got it all the way from my room to here and now you knocked it off," he whispered. I turned on the entrance-hall light and surveyed the scene. What I saw was: item one, Ape Face, tear-streaked and sweat-drenched; item two, the large lumpy something which turned out to be the Box; and item three, a skateboard attached to a rope.

"What's with the skateboard?"

"I was trying to get the set upstairs to Boris's, but it's too heavy so I thought I could balance it on the skateboard, but it keeps falling off. Anyway, now you're here, can't you carry it? Because it's almost six and I'm going to be late for the movie."

I sighed. "Okay, just give me two secs to change my sweater. And you better do a job on your face. It's all smudged from . . ." I tactfully refrained from finishing the sentence, but he knew what I meant.

"I wasn't crying. It was just that thing keeping falling off made me so mad, I got prespired."

"Sure. Anyway, it was a good idea; I never would have thought of it. Hurry up and get washed, and if you're done ahead of me, turn out the hall light and ring for the elevator."

"Gee, thanks, Annabel. I love you, Annabel," he said, cheerily trotting off to the bathroom. Doesn't take much to please him, thank heavens.

When I got back, the elevator was waiting and Ape Face was just stepping into it.

"No wonder you had trouble," I grumbled as I lurched in after him, staggering under the weight of our precious cargo.

"Say, what is this?" said Hector Wong, the afternoon man.

"What does it look like, a bunch of daisies? It's a television set," I gasped.

"That I could tell from looking. What I meant was what is this big traffic in TVs all of a sudden? Twelve o'clock I took your upstairs friend down with one, and now I'm taking you down with one."

"For one thing, it's none of your business, and for another, I don't want to go down, I want to go up."

"The kid buzzed the down," said Hector, reversing gears with stomach-sickening abruptness. "How was I to know?"

"The kid buzzed the down because he is a creature of habit and down is his usual route. However, we want up—to my upstairs friend's—and *quick*, por favor. It's heavy!"

Hector, being a Brooklyn-born Chinese Puerto Rican, is fluent in all three languages. When we're friends, which is most of the time, he's delighted to let me practice my Spanish on him, but today he seemed to be taking it as an ethnic slur.

"#%*°@+!" he said darkly in inscrutable Mandarin, and brought the car to a deliberately inept crash landing at the ninth floor. I sank to my knees and had to let him help me up.

"Muchas gracias por nada," I retorted, staggering into the Harris's elevator hall.

"Are you going to ring the doorbell for me, Ape Face, or do you want me to ring it with my nose?"

Ape Face giggled. "Ring it with your no . . ."

"Ring that bell or I'll drop this on your head!" I commanded.

Ape Face rang the bell. Nobody came.

"Ring it again. I'm dying," I said.

He did. Still nobody came. Ape Face put his ear to the door.

"I think I hear the maid vacuuming in there. Maybe she can't notice us."

"She'll notice this," I said, heaving my full weight (approximately two hundred and twenty pounds) against the door. Because it was already open, it instantly gave way, and I landed in the middle of the entrance hall, where I deposited the set on the floor with a resounding *thunk.*

In the living room the Hoover was going full blast, but no one was attached to it.

"Where's the maid?" asked Ape Face.

"I don't know, but she's bound to be somewhere."

"Hey, look! What's that?" he shrieked, pointing to two legs sticking out from under the sofa.

"The maid, I guess."

"Is she dead?"

"Of course not, silly. Her legs are moving. She must be cleaning under there."

"Why doesn't she come out and say hello?"

"Because she doesn't know we're here."

"Let's tell her," said Ape Face, advancing cautiously toward the sofa. "I'll give her a little tap."

"Don't do that!" I said, grabbing him by the arm. "You'll give her a heart attack. We'll just say hello—loudly. Ready? One, two, three. HELL-O!"

"I think she heard," said Ape Face. "I can see more of her now than I could before."

We watched, fascinated, as first the bottom, then the middle and shoulders and arms, and finally the face appeared. It didn't seem too undone at the sight of us—just puzzled.

"Hi, there," I said jovially.

"What? Wait a minute," said the maid. She scrambled to her feet, dumped a handful of pistachio-nut shells into an ashtray, smoothed down her white uniform, and turned off the Hoover.

"There. That's better. Now—what did you say?"

"I said Hi, here we are."

"So I see," she said, looking us up and down. "How did you get in?"

"You left the front door open. You know, you really shouldn't do that," I said sternly. "Somebody might walk in and steal something."

"Somebody like you, you mean?"

"Certainly not," I said indignantly. "I'm Annabel Andrews and this is my brother, Ben. We're friends of Boris's."

She looked dubious.

"I mean Morris's. I always call him Boris. Didn't he tell you we were coming?"

"No, but that's all right. Make yourselves comfortable."

Ape Face was tugging at my sleeve. "Can I ask you a secret? Where's the den? *The Mask of Dimitrios* is going to start."

"What's he want—the bathroom?" asked the maid.

"No, the den. Boris said he could watch a movie on the TV in there."

"That way," said the maid, pointing.

"Thank you," said Ape Face, and sauntered off.

"Cute kid," remarked the maid. "Now what can I do for you? Can I get you anything?"

"Oh no, thanks," I said, plumping myself down on the sofa. "I'll just wait here for Boris. You just go on with whatever you were doing."

"I'm finished with whatever I was doing," she said, plumping herself down on the sofa beside me. "Well, not *finished,* but finished—if you know what I mean."

A quick look around the living room and I knew exactly what she meant: Half the tables were covered with dust, the rug had flug on it, and every ashtray was filled with cigarette butts and pistachio-nut shells. And there sat the maid, pretty as you please, with her feet up on the coffee table! Maybe a tactful hint was in order.

"Are you sure I'm not interrupting you?" I asked.

"No, no," she said airily. "That's it for today. I hate housework, don't you?"

"Everybody hates housework," I said, trying not to sound sanctimonious, "but you shouldn't feel there's anything demeaning about it. After all, *somebody's* got to do it."

"I'd just as soon the somebody weren't me," she grumbled, and then abruptly changed the subject. "How about a drink?"

"I don't drink," I said stiffly, watching in horror as she drifted over to the bar and poured herself a Scotch. "And you shouldn't either," I blurted out. "It's not a good thing to do when you're working."

"Hell, no," she said in a bland tone. "But I've stopped working now, anyhow." Really, the woman was outrageous! I wondered if Boris and his mother had any idea what went on when they weren't there.

"Have you been working here long?" I asked.

"Only a couple of hours. The living room wasn't as bad as the kitchen."

"No, I mean have you been in this position long?"

"In this position long?" she repeated slowly, with a thoughtful frown.

Then, light suddenly dawned. "Oh, *now* I understand. You want to know if I've been in this *position* long." She hooted with laughter and sat down next to me on the sofa again.

"My dear, I've been in this position for ages. *Ages!* Does that surprise you?"

"Frankly, yes," I admitted. "Last year, we had a maid who drank. My mother fired her."

"Is that so?" She raised her eyebrows and looked at me owlishly. "Then it's a good thing I don't work for your mother, isn't it?"

"Darn right," I said in a steely tone.

There was an awkward silence. Then the maid said, "So you're a friend of Morris's. I'm glad to know he has one."

"He has plenty. He just never brings them home."

"So I've noticed. Why is that, do you suppose?"

Because thanks to you, his home is a disaster area, is what I was tempted to say. Instead, I said, "I don't know. Except maybe he doesn't want people to meet his mother. I get the impression he's not overly fond of her."

"I get that impression, too," she said, staring speculatively off into space.

"What's she like?" I asked curiously.

"Well, let's see now. How to describe her . . .? I guess you could do it in one word." She chuckled. "Crazed."

"Dangerously crazed?" Poor Boris!

"Oh no, I wouldn't say so. Just eccentric. Most writers are, you know."

"I didn't know she was a writer. Boris never mentioned it. What kind of stuff does she write?"

"Oh—poetry, books, magazine articles. Poetry, mostly."

"Is it any good?"

"I wouldn't know how to judge that."

"No, I suppose you wouldn't," I said, thinking *True Confessions* was probably more up her alley.

"And she's a lousy mother, right?"

"I wouldn't know how to judge that either. I guess she's a lousy mother for someone like Morris. He's sensible, she's not."

"Well, what do you think of her as a *person*? Is she nice?"

"Hard to say. She tries to be nice. Sometimes I like her, sometimes I don't. But she's very easy to work for," she added with a mischievous grin. "Nobody else in the world would put up with me."

"Oh, I don't know about that," I said politely. "You're not as conscientious as our maid, but you're quite interesting to pass the time of day with."

"Thank you. What time *is* it?" she said, glancing at her watch. "My God, I'm supposed to be somewhere by six thirty."

"But I thought you were staying to fix supper."

"Who me? Out of the question. If you get hungry, help yourself to whatever you want in the fridge. I'm going inside to change out of these rags."

While she was gone, I dusted off a few tables with my sleeve and emptied the ashtrays into a wastebasket. It was so messy in that room, even I couldn't stand it. I was just about to de-flug the rug when the maid reappeared, looking really quite attractive.

"What's it like out?" she asked, flinging open the hall closet door. "Too warm for fur?" *Now* what was she up to—borrowing Madame's clothes?!

"Much too warm for fur."

"Oh. Well, I'll wear this, then," she said, diving into a Bill Blass raincoat.

"Pardon me for asking, but is that yours?" I inquired.

"Yes," she said. "Pardon *me* for asking, but is *that*

yours?" she said, pointing to the television set.

"Boris's. I'm returning it."

"I thought it looked familiar. When he comes back, tell him to move it out of the hall before somebody breaks a leg." Rather bossy of her, it seemed to me.

"Is there anything else you want me to tell Boris?"

"Yes. Tell him to invite you back again soon. His mother would enjoy talking to you."

"How do you know?"

"I know," she said, chucking me under the chin. "I've been in this position a long time, remember?"

And with that, she flew out the door.

Fifteen minutes later, with the Ape's new Sony in a box under his arm, Boris flew in. And I really mean flew; I'd never seen him so excited.

"Annabel!" he shouted. "It's going to work! It's going to *work*!"

"I should hope so. It's brand-new, isn't it? Anyway, where've you been, what took you so long, and why didn't you call? We've been waiting for hours."

Boris babbled on, "I'm not talking about the Sony, I'm talking about the whole thing. The whole thing's going to work. Whole new horizons have opened up, my life is going to change, I'm going to be a billionaire! I tell you, it's going to work—I knew it all along!"

"Boris," I said impatiently, "slow up and calm down. I don't know what you're talking about."

"Listen to me. Are you listening?"

"I'm listening."

"All right: What do you think this Sony cost? Take a rough guess."

"A hundred and fifty?"

"Wrong. A hundred and sixty-seven ninety-nine. They've gone up. Now, what do you think I got for my Motorola?"

"A hundred and *seventy*-seven ninety-nine."

"Wrong! A hundred and five," said Boris with a broad smile. Unless my arithmetic was worse than I thought, he'd just lost money on the deal. What was he so happy about?

"According to my calculations, you're out approximately sixty dollars."

"Wrong again," said Boris, beaming from ear to ear. With a flourish, he produced a wad of greasy bills from his pocket and waved them under my nose. "A hundred and thirty-seven dollars profit I made today! Aren't you going to guess how?"

"No, I'm not," I said. "I'm tired of guessing wrong and I'm tired of playing twenty questions. You tell me."

"I bet the guy! The guy in the TV store. See, we had the trade all worked out and then I asked him if Monday was okay to pay him the extra sixty-two ninety-nine because I didn't have it on me, and he said nothing doing. It looked like the transaction was falling through.

"Then I noticed he had all the sets in the store

on—you know, to show how well they worked—and guess what was on? No, don't guess, I'll tell you: The Mets–Reds game. So, very casually, I got into a conversation with him about how I thought the Reds would win, easy. He told me I was off my rocker, so I bet him two hundred bucks. That's why I was late getting here; I had to wait 'til the game was over to collect. Boy, was he sore! Zowie!" he yelped with a final burst of enthusiasm, "Do I ever love this wrecked-up Box!"

"Charming," I said scornfully. "A charming display and a charming story. Taking advantage of a poor old man . . ."

"What poor old man? He was a middle-aged slob who would've taken advantage of *me* if I hadn't beat him to it! My Motorola was worth more than a hundred and five and he knew it. Come on, Annabel, help me carry the Box into my room; I want to catch the seven o'clock news."

"Two wrongs don't make a right. Carry it yourself. I lugged it up here, you can lug it the rest of the way."

Boris, still euphoric from his ill-gotten gains, said, "Fair enough." With a grunt, he hoisted it onto his shoulder, marched off with it, and returned, singing, "When I am a rich man, deedle, deedle, deedle, dydle, dydle, dah . . ."

"But Boris, it's not moral," I protested.

"I make it a rule," he said grandly, "never to discuss

morals on an empty stomach. What time is the maid serving dinner?"

"She isn't. She left."

"Left! Rats! I'm starving. Why did she leave?"

"I dunno. She said she had to be somewhere at six thirty."

"I bet that's the last we see of her," he said gloomily. "Cranky old bat."

"She didn't strike me as cranky—just unreliable. As a matter of fact . . ." I was about to enlighten him further, but he was already on his way to the kitchen, muttering, "I guess I'll have to whip something up myself again."

"In that case, maybe I'd better call home and see if Ape Face can eat there." I reached for the kitchen phone.

Boris snatched it out of my hand. "I wouldn't do that if I were you."

"Why not? Your mother can't object to a guest making one quick call." I snatched it back.

"Proceed at your own risk," said Boris sourly.

I did. There was no dial tone.

"That's funny," I said. "It's out of order or something."

"Or something," said Boris, replacing the receiver in the cradle. "Too bad for Ape Face. I'll have to make do with whatever I find in the fridge—as usual. And I shudder to think what. Probably nothing but a desiccated lemon, a jar of pressed caviar, and a mystery mold in a covered dish. Am I right?"

I opened the fridge door. There was a ton of gorgeous-looking food.

"You're *wrong*, for a change."

Boris peered over my shoulder. "Where did all that come from? Oh, yeah—my mother had a party last night."

"I thought she didn't cook."

"She doesn't. She orders it in from Sardi's at ten dollars a head."

"But look how much is left! Wow, what a waste!"

"Here, hold the plates; I'll serve. Lasagne?"

"Thanks."

"Turkey?"

"Thanks."

"Ham? Chutney? Rye bread? Brie?"

"Thanks." Pretty soon I stopped saying thanks and just let him heap it on. We set a plate down in front of Ape Face, who was glued to his movie in the den. Then we made our way back to Boris's room with roughly four heads' worth on our own plates, which we managed to dispose of in fifteen minutes of uninterrupted gorging. We had to start with the peach tart because it was piled on top, and work our way down to the lasagne and salmon canapés at the bottom. I tell you, it was positively revolting.

"Well, now that we've got that over with," I said, stifling a mammoth burp, "let's talk."

"Let's not," said Boris, turning on the set. "We've missed half the news already. Just as long as I'm in time for the sports, though.. . ."

In enforced silence, while Boris scribbled in his notebook, I watched the results of Sunday's ball game (the Giants won), and a tennis match in Phoenix (Rosemary Casals won). I found it pretty stultifying; but then, unlike Boris, I wasn't out to rip off the world.

"Can I talk now?" I said acidly.

"Sure," he said, turning off the set. "What do you want to talk about?"

"Well, for one thing, I'd like to know who you're going to find to take advantage of tomorrow. It's Sunday; there won't be any unsuspecting shopkeepers around."

"Are you going to start that again?! I told you I didn't want to discuss it."

"You said you didn't want to discuss it on an empty stomach. Now you've got a full stomach. And so have I. So let's discuss it. I think you're a greedy, avaricious, mean, amoral miser!"

"That's some discussion! More like character assassination."

"Then defend yourself!"

"I can't."

"Just what I thought!" I said triumphantly.

"I mean I don't want to," said Boris. "Please, Annabel, *please.* I have reasons I don't want to go into—so please can't we change the subject?" He looked ashamed and miserable.

"All right," I said, relenting. "If I can think of what to change the subject *to.*" My mind was a complete blank.

Finally I thought of something. "I know. Let's talk about your mother."

"Do we have to?" asked Boris uneasily. I glared at him. Resigned to his fate, he nodded. "What can I tell you?"

"Well, the maid said your mother was a writer. I never knew that."

Boris feigned nonchalance. "Oh yes. She's quite famous, old Sascha is."

"Sascha Harris? I've never heard of her."

"She uses the name Sascha Biegelman."

"Oh, Sascha *Biegelman.*"

"You've heard of her," said Boris delightedly.

"No, I haven't heard of her either." There's no point in lying about things like that; you always get caught.

"I thought from the way you said her name . . ." he trailed off, disappointed. "Biegelman is her pen name. She made it up," he added.

"Why Biegelman?"

"Would I know? She probably found it in the Yellow Pages under carpets. She found an analyst that way once."

"Under *carpets*?!"

"No, dummy. But she might just as well have, for all the good he did her. Three hours a week at forty-five dollars an hour for five years makes—let me see—approximately thirty-five thousand one hundred dollars down the drain."

"My Lord, Boris, you're a walking computer, aren't you! I had no idea you were so good at math."

"I have to be," he said grimly. "I didn't want to go into this—but as long as you've got me started—Would you like to see something?" He opened the bottom drawer of a file cabinet. "Look. Just look in there. You know what that is? Six years of bank statements and canceled checks. I've been balancing her checkbook ever since I was nine. And it's no picnic, let me tell you; she's overdrawn half the time, the ditz!"

He jerked open the middle drawer of the file cabinet. "You know what's in here? Monthly statements from the brokerage firm. A couple of years ago, she wanted to go on a thirty-seven-day Silk Screen and Ceramics tour of the Orient. When I reminded her she was into my school for twenty-five hundred and into the Feds for more than a thou for back taxes, she said, 'I can sell stock.' So I told her she didn't have any stock left to sell—which she believed because she's too sloppy to know what's what; and ever since then, I've been hiding her stock statements. I also hide her savings-account book. It's my hedge against bankruptcy."

"So she didn't get to go on the trip."

"Sure she did. A little problem like insufficient funds wouldn't stop Sascha. When I hit her with the good news about the stocks, she said, 'What the hell, Charley, you only live once, I'll sell the Picasso.' (My grandmother left her a Picasso.)

"The next day, she bopped into the Parke-Bernet gallery with the thing, made herself a deal, sent the big check to the Feds and half a dozen fairly big checks to charities; and a week later, she bopped off to the Land of the Rising Sun, leaving me to stare at an empty white rectangle on a dirty gray wall."

"Stupefying!" I said. "Simply stupefying!"

"Yeah, isn't it?" agreed Boris, mournfully. "And I loved that picture. It was a great picture. But that's not the worst. Wait'll you hear this: She never paid the school bill. Not that year, or this year either. They've been pretty nice about it, but they're not going to be much longer. In fact, they've already sent a letter saying they couldn't keep me next year 'unless,' et cetera, et cetera. From where I sit, 'unless' seems highly unlikely."

"My God, Boris, what will you do?"

"I don't know. I suppose I could go live with my uncle in California—the public schools are better out there than here—but I certainly wouldn't want to." Boris looked very morose, but not as morose as I felt. Boris in California? What a ghastly thought! Steady on,

Annabel, it hasn't happened yet.

"Not that I don't like my uncle. He's an okay enough guy; in fact, a very okay guy. But I really couldn't move to California even if I did want to because . . ." He ran down, deep in dire thoughts of doom and gloom.

"Because?" Any reason for Boris not to go to California was a reason I was anxious to hear.

"Well, because, don't you see? She's so helpless. She's such a totally irresponsible . . . a child, that's what she is. The money hassles are a perfect example. Her father, my Connecticut grandfather, he's a typical Yankee; you'd think some of that penny-saved-is-a-penny-earned stuff would have rubbed off on her, but maybe it traumatized her instead. All I know is if I didn't keep an eye on her, she'd spend every dime she earned. As it is, she does pretty well in the spending department."

He paced up and down nervously for a minute or so, and then abruptly wheeled around to face me head-on. "Listen," he said in a choked-up voice, "You want to hear something really lovely? You want to hear the lovely latest?"

"I don't know if I do," I said. Boris's recital was unnerving me terribly.

"Well, you're going to, whether you like it or not. Serves you right for bugging me about wanting to make money.

"That present I gave you—the walkie-talkie—I said

it was because Sascha wouldn't let me use the phone? Ha!" he sneered. "There *is* no phone. Not in operation, anyway, not right now. For the third time in two years, it's been cut off for nonpayment of bills. You know what you would've heard if you'd called up here in the last five days? 'I am sorry. The number you have reached is not in service at this time, or has been temporarily disconnected.' That's why I couldn't call you this afternoon. It's humiliating and horrible!"

He put his hands over his face and started to cry.

"Oh Boris, please Boris, don't! I can't bear it," I said, stricken.

"It's all right," he said. "I'll be all right in a second." He took a few deep breaths, and then straightened up and smiled wanly.

"That was dumb, wasn't it?"

"Not a bit," I assured him. "Furthermore, if I were in your shoes, I'd probably do the same thing."

"What else would you do if you were in my shoes? After six years of playing nursemaid to a nut, I'm getting pretty sick of my shoes."

"I can't say as I blame you."

"I mean it! What would *you* do?"

"I haven't the foggiest notion. It's a very complex problem, that much is obvious, and I couldn't come up with any quick answers. I haven't had enough time to think about it."

"Well, I have. Too much time. So last night, I made

a little list." From his pocket, he produced a crumpled sheet of paper. "This is a list of things I've decided my mother needs in her life and doesn't have. I'd like to read it to you, and if you have any other suggestions, please make them, okay?"

"Shoot."

"One: a good shrink. That's the most important. Nothing from the Yellow Pages—she's got to have a sympathetic but well-qualified type who knows how to create order out of chaos. Two: a new accountant. The one she has only does her tax forms and charges a fortune; I do everything else and I don't want to do it anymore. Three: a lot of new furniture and a new paint job. This place is falling-down disgusting; nothing's been done to it since the day we moved in. Four: all new equipment for the kitchen. Five: a decent housekeeper to cook in the kitchen and clean the house; I'm sick of TV dinners and fuzz under the bed. Six: a secretary to answer the phones, type manuscripts, and paste rave reviews into nice leather scrapbooks. Seven: a whole new wardrobe for Sascha and one decent sports jacket for me. Eight: twenty thousand dollars to clean up past debts and another fifty thousand in case there are future ones. That sounds like a lot, but if the new shrink isn't more successful than his predecessor, she won't be able to pay him the thirty-five thousand he'll charge for helping her with her money neurosis unless I hold something in reserve. That's all I've come up with so far," concluded Boris. "What do you think?"

I was beginning to enjoy myself. Boris's list reminded me of a game I used to play when I was a kid: If you found a million dollars lying in the gutter, how would you spend it?

"It's an extremely thorough list. You only forgot one item: a nice man."

"Oh, that. I didn't forget. But she had a nice man, once. My father. And she blew it—he left her. She'll probably never find another one," he added mournfully. "Unfortunately, it's something money can't buy. I wish it could."

"Never mind. I just thought there was no harm in mentioning it. After all, as long as we're in fantasy land, we might as well make it perfect."

"Who said anything about fantasy land?" he said indignantly. "This is a very real list to accommodate some very real needs." Dear God, he's going the way of his mother—stark, raving mad.

"Boris, you're on a trip. It may be a very real list, but it requires a heap of very real money. From whence, pray tell, are you going to get it?"

"From this whence right here," he said, patting the Box. "This same wonderful whence that brings you tomorrow's weather is going to bring me unlimited fortunes with which to pay for items one through eight."

"How? From betting on ball games with Chuckie Waterman, Charlie Kuchel, and innocent shopkeepers?"

"No. From betting on horses at OTB."

"Hey!" I said, admiringly. "I never thought of that. Aren't you the clever one. Like the Kentucky Derby—you could make a mint in one day." I was all excited.

"I don't want to make a mint in one day. Any time you win over six hundred dollars at once at OTB, it gets reported to the government and you have to pay income tax. It's better to make a mint in a lot of days—a little at a time. Like Aqueduct or Roosevelt, Monday through Saturday, month after month."

"Do they show the results of those races on television? I've never seen them."

"I vaguely remember they do. The trouble is I don't know when. It must be sometime in the afternoon or evening; I'll just have to keep switching channels 'til I catch it."

"Wouldn't it be easier to call OTB and ask them?"

Boris looked up in surprise. "It certainly would. Why didn't I think of that?"

I gave him a consolation pat on the shoulder. "Because you don't have a phone. Don't berate yourself. You can't be expected to think of everything."

"You know, Annabel," he said earnestly, "you could be a great help to me with all of this. I could really use you. Between us, we'd make a great team. If I promise not to take advantage of people like Chuckie Waterman and Harvey Kuchel (although if you knew Harvey Kuchel . . .)."

"Ah-ah-ah," I warned.

"All right, all right, forget Harvey Kuchel; he's penny-ante stuff anyway. But if I promise not to take advantage of people like that, will you help me?"

"How? You don't need me for betting. What else is there?"

"I don't know, offhand. But when I find out, will you help me?"

"If you'll help me," I said.

"Sure. But how?"

"Well," I said slowly, "this is going to sound kind of stupid . . ."

"That's nothing new," snickered Boris. He was back to his old self, I noted.

"Do you want me to help you or not?"

"Yes, I do. I'm sorry," he said promptly.

"Boris, remember when you made fun of me for not realizing the Box was good for more than just weather predictions? And then you explained how we couldn't prevent events from happening but we *could* benefit from advance information?

"Well, you want to benefit from advance information to change your mother's life—and yours, too. After what you've told me, I certainly don't blame you for that. But couldn't other people also benefit from advance information? I know this sounds sappy and idealistic, but take that freak blizzard, for instance. I'm built like a horse and being out in it didn't do me much harm; but suppose I had a little old frail grandmother who was going out for a walk that day. I'd want to warn her."

"Unless you gave the whole thing away, your little old frail grandmother wouldn't believe you any more than you believed your brother."

"Probably not, but I could persuade her to stay indoors. I could play gin rummy with her until the blizzard began and she saw for herself. By using that advance information, I might actually be saving her life.

"Or take another for instance: We see on the Box that a woman in Queens has had quintuplets—over three pounds each and all of them healthy. But the poor lady is frantic with worry because the doctors have told her to expect multiple births and she doesn't know how many—or whether they'll survive. Wouldn't it be fun to tell her everything was going to be okay?"

"Why would *she* believe you? She'd figure if the doctors didn't know, why should you?"

"Oh Boris, don't take me literally—I'm just winging these examples. All I know is I'm sure there's a use for the Box *besides* making money.

"So I want you to promise you'll tell me everything that shows up on the Box whenever I want to know. Will you promise?"

"On one condition: that you never reveal your source."

"I absolutely never will."

"All right. I promise. And in return, you promise to help me?"

"I promise." He threw his arms around me joyfully and kissed me (on the cheek).

"Annabel, you are a super person! *I* thank you, and my *mother* thanks you . . ."

"That's ridiculous."

"Well, she would if she knew. Although maybe it's lucky she doesn't; she doesn't know what's good for her anyway, she's such a crazy lady."

"The maid said she wasn't crazy—just eccentric."

"Is that what the maid said? Flora the Fink said that? Some nerve! It's one thing for me to criticize my mother and quite another for her to."

"Don't get ruffled. She wasn't criticizing—just analyzing. You know something, Boris? From the way you talk now, I can't figure out: Do you like your mother or do you hate her?"

"What's your guess?" Shrewd of him, wasn't it—trying to get me to give him the answer.

"I simply don't know," I said.

"I simply don't either. Sometimes I like her, sometimes I don't."

"The maid said the same thing."

Boris gave me a queer look. "What else did the maid say?"

"Let me see, now. She said your mother was easy

to work for—which is fortunate. She's a fiasco of a maid, you know."

"No, I didn't."

"Oh, yes, she's really frightful. *I'm* a better cleaner and that's not saying much."

"What else?" asked Boris curiously.

"Well, when I asked her if she thought your mother was a lousy mother, she said, 'Lousy for someone like Morris. He's sensible, she's not.'"

"She happens to be right; but how would she know a thing like that, I wonder."

"I suppose anybody who'd been around as long as she has could figure it out."

"Two weeks? I wouldn't call that long. Although, come to think of it, two weeks is *quite* a long time in our house. They usually leave sooner. Everything's so erratic, including the pay."

"Strange," I mused. "She gave me the feeling . . . No! She actually said, 'I've been in this position for ages.' And then she giggled."

"Tell me more," insisted Boris.

"I don't want to get her in trouble. She was very pleasant, really."

"More," he demanded.

"Well," I said hesitantly, "she drinks. Helped herself to a slug of Scotch."

"No kidding! Tsk, tsk, tsk!"

"Yes. And when she changed out of her uniform,

she did it in the master bedroom. And then she put on a coat from the hall closet. I told her it was too warm for fur so she put on a good raincoat. I thought maybe it was your mother's and I asked her, but she said it was hers."

"I think I'm beginning to get the picture," said Boris. "Tell me, did the coat fit?"

"Perfectly. Why?"

"Was this maid about fifty-five years old and fat and spoke with a Spanish accent?"

"No! She was about forty years old, thin, and spoke plain English."

"Annabel," said Boris, howling with laughter, "that was no maid—that was my mother!"

I wanted to die on the spot. Since that wasn't possible, I did the next best thing: fled from it. It was like a Mack Sennett ballet. Without so much as a good-bye to Boris, I tore into the den, wrested my glassy-eyed brother away from *The Partridge Family,* stuffed the new Sony into a shopping bag (for purposes of concealment), rang the elevator bell, decided not to wait for the elevator, galloped down the back stairs to our apartment, dragged Ape Face to his room, hid the Sony in the toy chest under the Lego, shouted "Hello, we're back, I'm tired, good night" to my parents, ripped off my clothes, dived into bed, pulled the covers over my head—and nearly burned up with embarrassment. (*There's* an interesting headline for Bartholomew

Bacon: GIRL'S FACE SETS SHEETS ON FIRE!)

Until nearly dawn, I tossed around looking for a cool place on the pillow, and attempted to reconstruct the scene with Sascha. I must have sampled practically every emotion in the book: Rage—what a rotten trick, leading me on like that!; hope—maybe she never knew I thought she was the maid; despair—she knew. It was obvious I didn't think she was the mother. Who else would she be?; bafflement—if she knew, why didn't she stop me from making a fool of myself? Was she simply trying to spare my feelings?; panic—what about *her* feelings? That awful thing I said about Boris not liking his mother!; curiosity—but actually she didn't seem surprised. She even admitted she wasn't a good mother for him. Why *did* she admit that, she didn't have to?; admiration—because she's honest about herself; despair—she must think I'm an idiot. I bet she hates me; hope—wait a minute! When she left, she said to tell Boris to invite me back because his mother would enjoy talking to me; wonderment—she *doesn't* hate me. In spite of it all, she likes me. I like her, too; determination—I'm going to apologize the first chance I get; relief—I'm falling asle . . .

Sunday, April 21

BEEP, BEEP, BEEP

I opened one eye and looked at my watch. Nine o'clock. Too early for beeping. I ignored it. Then there was more beeping. In a stupor, I reached for the walkie-talkie and shoved it with my feet to the bottom of the bed. No dice; the covers muffled the sound but the vibrations were tickling my toes. I fished it back up again and punched the talk button.

"Whaddya want?" I croaked.

"Good morning. This is the butler speaking."

Har-de-har-har!

"Boris the Butler calling Annabel. Are you there, Annabel?"

"No." I clicked off and rolled over. On four hours' sleep, what I didn't need was a little light banter with Boris the Butler. What I needed was more sleep. I closed my eyes and tried for it; but waiting for the walkie-talkie to blast at me was like waiting for the other shoe to drop. When it didn't, I wondered why not, and the wondering kept me awake.

I beeped Boris impatiently, four or five times.

"Sh," he cautioned. "One of those is enough. The 'maid' is working on a sonnet. Or a novel. I forget which."

"Boris, if you have any sensitivity whatsoever, you will drop that extremely painful subject and never refer to it again."

"I don't know why you're so upset about it—I'm sure she isn't. But all right, *Sascha* is working on a sonnet or a novel, I forget which. Is that better?"

"Much," I said, mollified. "What did you beep me for?"

"To tell you I can't see you today. I'm working on my plan for Sascha—adding up the figures on that itemized list."

A Sunday without Boris? Unthinkable! My feelings were hurt.

"That's all right, Boris," I said stoically. "I'll make my own plans. Did you watch the late news last night?"

"Yes. Why?"

"Is anything interesting happening today?"

"Mmmn . . . they caught the hijackers."

"Where?"

"In Cairo." No good—too far away.

"Any local news—fires, murders, quintuplets?"

"A shoot-out on Lenox Avenue in Harlem."

"Lenox Avenue and where?"

"At 127th Street, I think. At two fifteen. Two dead and one wounded. Let's see—what else? Sports you saw yesterday; the balmy weather turned blustery after lunch, and *Catch as Catch Can* opened at the Sutton Cinema; the critics loved it. What kind of good deed are you going to get out of all that?"

"I don't know yet, but I'll think of something. Good-bye."

I clicked off and went over today's events in my mind. The only thing that sounded promising was the shoot-out; but since I couldn't prevent it, what could I do with it?

Suddenly, for some reason (possibly having to do with his beautiful smile and his cute nose), a vision of Bartholomew Bacon popped into my head. A reporter could benefit from it.

With Bartholomew Bacon's card in my hand, I tiptoed to the kitchen phone. My parents were still asleep—but in case they woke up, I didn't want to be overheard.

The *Daily News* number range eleven times and was finally answered by a grunt.

"Bartholomew Bacon, please," I said in a businesslike tone.

"Snot innaday."

"Excuse me?"

"Bacon . . . snot . . . innaday," said the grunt, articulating carefully.

"Oh dear. It's vital that I get in touch with him. Could you give me his home number? This is an emergency."

"Unh," grunted the grunt. "Hold on. Bacon, Bacon. 555-4382."

I thanked him, hung up, took a swig of orange juice from the carton in the fridge, and headed back for the phone. I could see it was going to be a long day.

Bacon's number rang only five times and was answered by a groan.

"Is this Bartholomew Bacon?"

"I think so. Check me around noon. I may know more by then. G'night."

"Wait a minute, don't hang up. This is Ann Smith. Remember me? Ann Smith? Marvin the Torch?"

"Oh, yes, sure. What's up—outside of me, that is?" He yawned loudly for my benefit. The nit—I can take a hint without sound effects!

"Should I call back later?"

"Nope. I'm up now. Once I'm up, I'm up. How did you get my number?"

"The paper. I told them it was an emergency. You said to call if something occurred to me. . . ." I heard Dad's voice in the hall. In a second, he'd be in the kitchen to start coffee.

"Listen, I can't talk now, but I do have some interesting information. Do you want to meet me for coffee in a couple of hours?"

"Make it one o'clock."

"Fine. Where? Just name the place."

"Three fifty-three West 52nd."

"What's way over there—a bar?"

"I live there. Fourth floor walk-up." Uh-oh. I didn't like the sound of that!

"Couldn't we meet at your corner drugstore?"

"Miss Smith, honey, today is my day of rest. I'm not stirring from my pad."

"But . . ."

"Morning, darling," said Dad. It was too late for buts.

"Okay, I'll be there. Good-bye. Morning, Dad. That was Virginia," I explained.

"Virginia. Is she the pretty one or the nasty one?" After all these years, he still can't keep my friends straight.

"Both. I have a date with her this afternoon." I didn't, of course, but I was going to have to manufacture one in order to account for my time; because although my parents are reasonably liberal, I had a feeling they wouldn't approve of me going to a strange man's pad on West 52nd Street.

When Dad left the kitchen, I called Virginia. She chewed me out royally for abandoning her on Bleecker

Street, and when she'd finally wound down, I apologized meekly and profusely.

Then I said, "Virginia, will you do me a huge favor?"

"It depends," she said cagily.

"I'm going somewhere this afternoon I don't want my parents to know about. If I tell them I'm with you, will you cover for me?"

"Where are you going?" My mother walked into the kitchen and started frying bacon.

"I can't say. Wait a minute, I'll take it in the study." I picked up the phone in the study, hung up the phone in the kitchen, and ran back to pick up the phone in the study. By the time I got there, Dad had settled into the armchair with the Sunday *Times*.

"Virginia?"

"What kind of secret?"

"Juicy."

"But you won't tell me? Nuts to you, luv." I looked over at Dad. He seemed engrossed in the paper.

"Virginia," I whispered, "There is absolutely *no privacy* in this madhouse."

"Then pop on over here, sweets. Our flat's silent as a tomb." Virginia is the most persistent person in the whole entire world!

"All right. You win. I'll be over around eleven thirty."

"Right-i-o. I'll make us a nice pot of tea. Ta-ta, ducks."

Ta-ta, yourself!

• • •

To tell Virginia the truth was clearly impossible. The Box had to remain a secret. There was only one thing I could tell Virginia: a big fat lie. I didn't have one prepared, but I'm pretty good at fabricating on my feet; all I had to do was let her ask me a few leading questions and something would undoubtedly come to mind.

"Well, now, Annabel," she said, gracefully pouring me a cup of Constant Comment, "what's this all about?"

"You'll never guess," I said mysteriously.

"You're going to sneak into an X-rated movie?" Not a bad idea; unfortunately, I couldn't think of the name of a single one; if she asked me, I'd be stuck.

"No. Guess again."

"You're going to that funky coffeehouse we passed on Christopher Street yesterday—where the avant-garde poets hang out."

That wasn't a bad idea, either, but if I said yes she might decide to come with me.

"No. Keep going."

"You've got a date?"

Beautiful! Beautiful, and not altogether untrue. "That's it exactly."

"A date with a *man*?" she asked incredulously.

"Of course, what else?" I gazed serenely at her.

Virginia set her teacup down gently on the table

and leaned toward me. In a hushed and solemn tone, she handed me my lie on a silver platter.

"Annabel, my dear, are you in love?" I lowered my eyes in becoming modesty and allowed a shy smile to cross my face—you could've hung me in the Louvre alongside the *Mona Lisa.*

"Yes, Virginia," I murmured softly, "I am."

"Oh, Annabel," she squealed, "I'm *thrilled* for you! Absolutely thrilled. Look at you—you're blushing!"

I hate people who tell you're blushing. Unless you get up and inspect your face in the mirror there's no way to know whether it's true or not. Furthermore, I bet most of the time it isn't; it's just something people love to say.

"I'm not blushing."

"You are, you are," she insisted. "Annabel, I want to hear all about him. Have you known him long?"

"Not very. Only a couple of weeks. It's been sort of a whirlwind romance." Virginia moaned in ecstasy.

"What does he look like?" I told her. More moans.

"He sounds divine. Where does he go to school?"

"He doesn't. I mean he's out of school. He's older, you see."

Naturally, Virginia wanted to know how old. I told her twenty-four. She was very impressed. Then she wanted to know where I'd met him, which was rather a sticky wicket. Where *would* a fourteen-year-old girl meet a twenty-four-year-old man? I hadn't been to any dances or parties lately, I couldn't say I'd met him through my parents. . . . For lack of anything better, I decided to go with the truth.

"Actually, I met him on the street. We bumped into each other and got to talking, and, well—that's how it all began. He's a newspaperman."

"A newspaperman?" Virginia curled her lip ever so slightly. "No wonder you don't want your parents to know."

"Not that kind of a newspaperman. He's a reporter. On the *Daily News.*"

"Oh, what a relief! I'd hate to see you bumming around with a delivery boy."

"Virginia, you're a terrible snob."

I then proceeded to extol at great length the various virtues of Bartholomew Bacon—without giving his name, of course: honest, kind, humorous, intelligent, college graduate, fine old Yankee family, a sister married to a Presbyterian clergyman—the works.

When I got through, Virginia wanted to know why I had to keep him a secret from my parents if he was all that wonderful. Clever question. But I had a clever answer ready. "Because the difference in our ages would worry them," I said.

"It worries me, too," said Virginia, the mother hen. "Let me give you one good piece of advice: No matter how honorable you think his intentions are, don't let him get you alone in his apartment. Where are you meeting him this afternoon?"

I couldn't resist. "In his apartment."

"Well," she said with an exaggerated sigh, "I just hope you know what you're doing. Don't forget, as your sole confidante, which I trust I am . . ." she looked questioningly at me.

"Absolutely," I assured her. Virginia always wants an exclusive on secrets.

"That's good. It wouldn't do to have everybody and his aunt knowing about it. Anyway, as your sole confidante . . ."

"And cover," I added.

"As your sole confidante and cover, I'm carrying a grave responsibility. If anything bad ever happened, I'd feel awful."

"Don't worry, it won't," I said, getting up to leave.

"What'll I do if your mother calls?"

"Can't you go out? Then if she calls, she'll think we're both out. Which we will be. I'll tell you what: Go see that great new movie at the Sutton—*Catch as Catch Can.*"

"Never heard of it."

"Go see it. By tomorrow, there'll be lines around the block. The critics . . . um—" Whoops! "—are going to love it—I feel it in my bones. And speaking of bones, wear a warm coat. It's nice out now, but it'll probably get colder." Two good deeds for Virginia.

"Right-i-o, pet," said Virginia, opening the front

door for me. "And Annabel, I hope I didn't sound stuffy. I'm really very, very happy for you."

"Me, too," I said.

"By the way, what are you going to do about your boyfriend Boris?"

"Nothing. He's not my boyfriend anyway. I mean, I like him, but I don't love him," I said, crossing my fingers. It was the only lie I regretted telling.

Sunday, April 21, later

BARTHOLOMEW BACON'S BROWNSTONE was a dilapidated dump. Full of garbage and bad smells in the vestibule and peeling paint in the halls. Endless flights of sloping stairs (no elevator), and a bannister too splintery to touch. I began to have misgivings.

On the fourth floor, there were two apartments, neither of which seemed to be right, judging by the names under the doorbells. One said Krasny (Mrs. Helen), the other said Bacchante. Hm. Now what? Maybe I was on the wrong floor.

I stood around for a while, trying to screw up enough courage to ring one of the two doorbells and ask about Bacon. Then, I stood around some more, trying to figure out whose was the safer doorbell to ring. For all I knew both Krasny and Bacchante were murderers. Finally, I opted for Krasny, on the theory that a woman murderer would be easier to defend myself against, but she wasn't home. Bacchante was, though. I could hear music playing; so after offering up a silent prayer that Bacchante was also a woman, I pushed the bell and peered through the peephole. I couldn't see a thing, of course; you never can.

The music stopped, I heard footsteps come to the door, then—silence. Well, here we are, I thought giddily. Me and a potential murderer with nothing separating us but a one-inch slab of wood and two giant locks which will be unbolted any second.

I took a deep breath. "Hello?"

"Yeah," said a gruff male voice.

"Mr. Bacchante?"

"Yeah."

"I'm sorry to bother you, but could you tell me what floor Bartholomew Bacon lives on?"

"Sure thing," said a friendly, familiar voice. Were there two people there, or was it a case of Jekyll and Hyde?

After endless fumbling, clicking, turning, and twisting, the door opened a tiny crack, revealing one green eye, half a mouth, half a cute nose, and half a head of Bartholomew Bacon's carrot-red hair.

"Oh, it's you," he said, sounding relieved.

"You took the words right out of my mouth."

"Are you alone?"

"Yes. Are you?"

"Yes. Wait'll I undo the chain and the police lock."

"You were expecting me, weren't you? Why all the

safety precautions?" I asked when he finally let me in.

"You never know. Can't be too careful around here; it's a rough neighborhood. But once I've got my barricade set up, it's not easy to break in here."

"It's also not easy to break out," I commented.

Bacon laughed. "That, too. Sometimes it takes me a good ten minutes to unscramble the locks. Have a seat. Sit anywhere."

It was a one-room apartment (bathtub in the kitchen type); my choice of anywhere was a chair with sprung springs or the bed. I chose the chair.

"Your voice sounded so funny at first. I thought I was in the wrong place."

"Nope. I talk like that to discourage unwelcome visitors."

"Is that why you have the wrong name under the doorbell, too?"

"That's not a wrong name. It's my name. Bartolomeo Bacchante," he said proudly. "I changed it to Bartholomew Bacon for purely professional reasons. Why did you change yours, Miss Smith?"

"I didn't," I stammered. "Ann Smith is my real name. Really."

"Okay," he said shrugging. "That's your story, you stick to it."

He reached for a pencil and pad from the desk and sat down at my feet.

"Now," he said briskly, "what's the rest of it?"

"The rest of what?"

"Your story. That's what you're here for, isn't it? To give me some dope on the Bleecker Street fire?" He waited expectantly, pencil poised.

"Uh . . . no, not exactly."

"No?! Then what *are* you here for? Gee whiz, you wake me up at the crack of dawn on my day off, get my hopes up about a hot lead—and I need one in the worst way—and then you haven't got anything to tell me?!" He scrambled to his feet and strode angrily to the window and back.

"I cleaned the place up for you and everything. Washed the cups, made coffee, made the bed. . . ." He glared at me. "Listen, Ann Smith. You're not Ann Smith. You're not eighteen years old. And that address you gave me is a phony, too. I checked it out."

"I thought you might. That's why I gave it to you. You struck me as being a very thorough person. I bet you're a good reporter."

"Flattery will get you nowhere. Yes, I'm a good reporter, but only when I have something to go on. At the rate I'm going now, I'll *never* get my own byline, let alone the Pulitzer Prize."

"Bart, I don't know anything more about the Bleecker Street fire than I've already told you; but I *do* know something that would make a sensational story for you. At two fifteen this afternoon, a vicious crime is going to be committed."

Bart looked nervous. "Are you involved in it?" Heavens, I hadn't thought of that!

"Oh no, not remotely." Thinking fast, I said, "I have ESP."

"Oh yeah? Prove it. Close your eyes." I did, dreading what was coming next. "I have a pack of cards in my hand. Now, I'm holding up one card. What suit is it?"

I opened my eyes. "I have a different kind of ESP. It doesn't work for cards."

"Nonsense. ESP is ESP. You've either got it or you don't. Close your eyes again. What suit am I holding up?"

I had a one-in-four chance of making it. "A spade."

"A heart. Now, I'm writing down a number between one and ten. What's the number?"

"Two?"

"Ten. You couldn't be farther away. Aah," he said disgustedly, "you don't have ESP. I wish you did. It would make a good story. Boy, do I need a good story. I haven't come up with anything decent in weeks; if I don't get something soon, they'll probably transfer me to the Women's Page—or fire me. One's almost as bad as the other. ESP my foot!"

"Then how did I know about that explosion on Bleecker Street? Because I did, you know. I had nothing to do with it whatsoever, but I was there ahead of time, waiting for it." Bacon's eyes widened in surprise.

"I *knew* it was going to happen. I also *knew* the Mets were going to lose yesterday, and I know the Giants are going to win today. *And*," I said, pausing for full dramatic effect, "I do know about something happening at two fifteen this afternoon which I'll be delighted to tell you about *if*."

"If what?"

"*If* you take me with you."

"Since you're the only one who knows where it is, I don't have much choice in the matter, do I?"

"Is your camera loaded?" He nodded. "Come on, then. If we hurry, we'll just make it."

We tumbled down the stairs, grabbed a cab, and arrived at 127th Street and Lenox at ten past two.

"I don't see anything," said Bart. "Everything looks normal."

"Wait," I said, crouching behind a mailbox. "Duck down. It'll be any minute now."

"I feel like a jerk," he complained.

"You won't in a minute. Better safe than sorry. Sh."

"I hope you're right. Hey, Ann," he whispered. "Why are you doing this for me?"

"I plan on being a journalist myself one day. I took pity on you." It was the only excuse I could think of. Besides, it was true.

"Oh."

"Get your camera ready."

"It is. But I don't know what to focus on." Neither

did I. Boris hadn't given me any details.

Then I saw a couple of thuggy-looking guys sidle up to a drugstore, nod furtively to each other, and walk in.

"Over there," I pointed. "That must be it."

That was it all right. Bullets, screams, police cars, ambulance sirens—it was a crime reporter's dream and Bart caught it all—including a good clear shot of the escaping robber and several close-ups of the dead robber in the doorway. According to Boris, though, there were two dead and one wounded. Where were the others?

"Bart, see that cop sitting down, leaning against the side of the building—do you think he's hurt?"

"Cops don't usually lounge around in the middle of a gunfight. I suppose he must be."

"Why don't you ask him?"

"I'm going to. Maybe he'll give me an interview." We walked over to the cop.

"Hey, buddy, are you hurt?"

"Just a leg wound. Nothing serious." Two down and one to go.

"I'm from the *Daily News.* Feel like telling me what happened?"

"Nothing much to tell. Fairly routine stuff. Two junkies ripping off a drugstore."

I muttered to Bart, "Ask him if somebody else besides the junkie got killed."

"Why?"

"Because my ESP tells me there are two dead and one wounded. The body count doesn't add up right, yet."

"Whew," whistled Bart. "You're a regular ghoul, aren't you."

"I'm a budding professional. *Ask* him."

"Hey, buddy, were there any other casualties?"

"Yeah. The owner of the drugstore got shot." Three down and none to go.

The cop got to his feet and limped off to a nearby squad car. Obviously, he was only the wounded one.

Just then, two ambulance attendants came out of the drugstore carrying a man on a stretcher. A woman, his wife, I guess, was hurrying along beside them, sobbing.

"Take it easy, lady," said one of the attendants. "Your husband's going to be fine. He's got good blood pressure, he's fully conscious—see? He wants to say something to you."

They stopped walking to let her hear. "Belle? Don't worry, Belle. I'm going to make it."

"Is he?" she asked tearfully. "Is he really?"

"There's no reason why not," said the attendant. "The bullet just nicked him a little is all. They'll patch him up in the emergency room and he'll be home tonight, for sure."

Suddenly, it hit me how horrible it all was.

"They shouldn't *tell* her that!" I said fiercely, fighting back my own tears. "They shouldn't get her hopes up—it'll only make it harder."

"Annie, Annie, hang on there," Bart said. "The guy looked pretty healthy to me. Look at his wife *now.* Full of smiles. If she believes the men, why shouldn't you?"

"Because I *know:* two dead and one wounded. *I know!*"

"Maybe your ESP is wrong this time."

"It's not. I tell you it's not!" I shrieked at him. "That poor lady. She thinks everything's terrific; but she's going to get a phone call in the middle of the night and there won't be anybody with her to comfort her or keep her company. You've got to *do* something! I did something for you, now you do something for me!"

"I'll do anything you want if you'll just stop screaming," he said anxiously. "What do you want me to do?"

"I want you to go find someone to stay with that poor old lady."

"Right," he said obediently, and disappeared into the crowd.

"All done," he said when he returned.

He took my arm. "Annie, you may not want to give me your correct name or age, but you're going to have to give me your address because I'm taking you home, right now."

He hailed a cab and got in with me.

"One Fifteen Central Park West," I said sniffling.

He handed me his handkerchief. "You know, you're not a ghoul at all. You're a marshmallow. Soft and sweet." I eked out a feeble smile.

As the cab pulled up in front of my building, he said, "I guess it was pretty rough on you, but I'm awfully grateful for this story. If you get any other flashes of ESP will you call me?"

"Sure. But I'm not coming with you to any more murders."

"I think that's a wise decision."

"'Bye, Bart."

"'Bye, Annie."

Monday, April 22

THE NEXT MORNING, before I left for school, I beeped Boris.

"Well, at last," he grumbled. "Where *were* you all afternoon?"

"Out. Out with Virginia. Where were you all evening?"

"Out with Virginia."

"You're kidding," I gasped.

"I called her to ask if she knew where you were; she said you'd been by earlier but you'd left. I've always thought she was snooty, but she was very friendly on the phone, so I invited her to the movies. Or maybe she invited me—I can't remember exactly who asked who."

Son of a gun! Talk about not letting the grass grow under your feet!

"I hope you had a nice time," I said frostily.

Boris was casual. "It was okay. After spending most

of the day working over figures, it was at least a welcome diversion.

"Listen—I have two big things to report: First of all, I found out which channel shows the racing results: Channel 5 on the ten P.M. news. Secondly, there's a sensational new development. Sascha is leaving for California on the eight o'clock plane tonight. She'll be gone a couple of weeks and maybe more. While she's away, I can get a great head start on the apartment—throw out all the old stuff, buy some new stuff, get the place painted. Which reminds me, do you know the name of a good painter?"

"No, but my mother keeps a list of people like that. I'll look it up for you. Boris, how are you going to pay for all this? You don't have any money yet."

"No problem. I told Sascha I needed some clothes and got her to give me all her credit cards plus a letter saying I have permission to charge. (Out of all those cards, her credit ought to be still good on one or two of them.) By the time the bills come in, I'll have made enough from OTB to pay them."

"Hmm," I said. "I hope you're right. Sounds risky to me."

"Don't be such a worrywart, Annabel. I'm very optimistic—in fact, I'm raring to go. Can you look up the name of the painter for me now?"

"I'll be late for school. How about this afternoon?"

"That'll do, I guess. Try me around five; before

that, I'll be out. I'm going to take the money I won Saturday to the main office of the telephone company to get our phone out of hock which will probably take me the rest of the afternoon. And then tomorrow I'll go over to the OTB on 72nd and Broadway and bet whatever's left on whoever's going to win."

"Lotsa luck."

"Who needs luck?" he said gleefully. "Luck doesn't even enter into it. Roger, over, and out."

I collected my books and went to say good-bye to my parents. They were reading the *Times,* and Ape Face was sprawled on the floor, poring over "Dick Tracy."

"Hey, Ape Face, can I look at the *News* for a minute?"

"When I've finished the comics."

"That'll take all morning," I said, snatching it away from him. He howled in protest and Ma said, "Annabel, that's extremely rude. Give it right back to him."

"In a minute," I said, staring at the front page which had an electrifyingly graphic picture of the dead robber and a brief account of the holdup. Continued on page 5.

"Annabel, I said give it *back* to him! Now!"

"Wait, wait! I just want to see one quick thing."

I turned to page 5 and hastily scanned the article. The second-to-last paragraph told me what I didn't want to know—but knew already: "Harry Steinberg, owner of the drugstore, died of a heart attack on the way to the hospital. His wife, Belle . . ."

"Here, *take* your stupid paper!" I said, flinging it at Ape Face.

"Somebody got out on the wrong side of the bed this morning," Dad said archly.

"That's an original statement if ever I heard one. Ape Face, are you coming? Because I'm leaving."

As we went out the door, I heard Dad say, "What's her problem?"

"She's just a typical adolescent," sighed my mother. (They always blame *everything* on that; it makes me *sick*!)

"Buenos Días," said Hector.

"Morning." I jabbed Ape Face in the ribs. "Where's your manners? Say good morning." Ape Face obliged.

"The señorita is angry today?"

"At me," said Ape Face.

"Pobrecito." Hector clucked sympathetically.

"Hector, talk English, will you?"

"Pobrecito means poor little kid."

"I already know that, thank you."

"Just trying to be helpful," he said, opening the elevator door. Ape Face scampered down the hall.

"Well, you're not," I retorted. Hector closed the door in my face.

By the time I'd arrived at school, I was in a thoroughly foul temper: mad at the world because of Harry Steinberg, mad at Ape Face because I'd been mean to him, and mad at Hector because he'd *seen* me be mean to him; and as for my adorable friend, Virginia, mad wasn't the word. Kill was more like it. I made a firm resolution not to talk to her unless I absolutely had to.

On the way home, I absolutely had to; there was no way to avoid it—we were on the same crosstown bus. She plunked herself down next to me and said, "Is anything wrong?"

I gazed out the window. "No, not at all."

"You've been avoiding me all day. You didn't even sit next to me in algebra." (I always sit next to her in algebra—she feeds me the answers. Today, I'd let her archenemy, Francine, feed me the answers.)

I shrugged. "Francine asked me first."

Virginia made another attempt. "How was your date?"

"Wonderful, thank you." I looked at her accusingly. "How was yours?"

The soul of innocence, she said, "Annabel, I'm thunderstruck! Is that why you're mad at me—because I went out with Boris? Why should you be mad at that?"

"Because you're my best friend—supposedly."

"But you're in love with another man! You spent an

hour telling me how divine he was. And you also told me very specifically that Boris was not your boyfriend. How can you possibly object to my going out with him? Really, ducks, you're a dog in the manger."

"And you're an ambulance chaser! The body was hardly cold in the grave before you couldn't wait to snatch it."

"That's unfair. Besides, I didn't call him—he called me."

"He called you to find out where *I* was," I pointed out.

"And where *were* you? Out with another man. Annabel, you're not being logical." She had me there.

"Maybe not," I admitted.

"If it's any comfort to you, Boris isn't even my type. I mean, he's very good-looking and all that—but he's too serious. Also, he's stingy; he made me pay for my own movie. So let's not talk about it anymore. Let's talk about something fun: How *was* your date?"

I was feeling better; it was time to let her off the hook. I rolled my eyes. "My date was super."

"Why don't you come home with me? There's chocolate cake. We can eat and you can tell me all about what's-his-name. Incidentally, what *is* his name?" That's what I need! I thought. Next thing I know, she'll be going out with him, too.

"What's-his-name will do nicely."

"You don't trust me?" she asked in an injured tone.

"Only as far as I can throw you," I said good-naturedly. "Listen, Virginia, I'd love to come home with you, but I have an errand to do." Which I did—look up the painter for Boris. "Here's my stop. I've got to get off." I decided to throw her a bone. "By the way, do you get the *Daily News*?"

"Yes."

"Read this morning's front-page story; what's-his-name wrote it and took all the pictures."

"How fabulous!" she exclaimed.

I blew her a kiss and jumped off the bus.

Boris didn't answer my beep at a quarter to five, or at five, or even at five fifteen. I hoped nothing had gone wrong with his plans. At five thirty, I wrote the painter's name and number down on a piece of paper and rang the elevator bell.

Patrick Sullivan, a big, fat, jolly guy, was on duty.

"Would you please deliver this envelope to Morris Harris?"

"I'll take it, Pat."

I nearly fainted dead away: Out from behind fat Pat stepped none other than Sascha Biegelman.

"Hello!" she said cordially. "Nice to see you again."

I was speechless.

"You are Annabel, aren't you? I'm—"

"I know," I said, bug-eyed with horror. "I know who you are—now."

"Well, do come in. I mean, come up. Come up and

we'll have a drink. A Coke for you, a drink for me, 'Can't you see how happy we will be,'" she concluded musically.

I hesitated. Fat Pat was worried. "Will it be in or out, Miss? I have a call on ten."

"In," said Sascha decisively. I stepped in.

"'Tea for two and two for tea,'" she sang on our way up in the elevator. "I forgot my key, do-dee," she sang in the elevator hall. "But the door's open anyway, unless Morris locked it when he left. Oh goody, he didn't."

I followed her into the apartment. She peered in the ice bucket. "Oh dear. No ice. It doesn't matter to me—I don't really want a drink; but I can get some out if you care. Do you?"

Wordlessly, I shook my head.

"Here you are, then," she said, handing me a warm can. "Come on in the bedroom and keep me company while I pack. I'm going to L.A. tonight—did Morris tell you?"

I nodded yes.

"You're a veritable Chatty Cathy today. Why so shy, all of a sudden?" She smiled at me encouragingly.

"Listen, Mrs. uh . . ." Harris? Biegelman? *Ms.* Biegelman?

"Sascha."

"I owe you an apology."

"Do you? What for?"

"You know what for. For thinking you were the maid."

She laughed. "A perfectly natural error. I was dressed like one." That's right, she was. No wonder I was confused. If she'd been dressed like a mother, I would have known.

"It was very embarrassing. In fact, it still is. Why did you do it?"

"If you're going to scrub kitchen floors and go foraging under sofas for pistachio nuts, a nylon uniform is the most practical thing to wear. Besides, I'm a writer; writers need to know how other people live. So, when the maid didn't show up, I thought: What the hell, *I'll* be the maid and see what that feels like—maybe I'll learn something."

"Did you?"

"Yes. It's boring. It's the most unengrossing work in the world. But, as you said yourself, a job's a job; there's nothing demeaning about it. Didn't you say that?"

"Yes. Plus a whole lot of other things I wish I hadn't said. All those things about Boris." I gave an involuntary shudder. "I want to apologize for them, too."

Sascha began heaving clothes onto the bed. "Look, Annabel, you don't owe me any apologies. It was dirty pool—what I did to you. But by the time I realized, the joke had gone too far, I didn't know how to stop it without making you feel worse. Furthermore, there was nothing you said about Boris, I mean Morris—" She laughed. "Now you've got me doing it. Actually, why not? I think I like the name Boris. It has a nice Russian sound to it. . . . Well, to continue, there was nothing you said about Boris I didn't already know. I know he can't stand me," she tossed a bunch of underwear and an armload of dresses and pants into a suitcase.

"I think that's overstating it a bit," I said judiciously.

"Well, his feelings are at best ambivalent, wouldn't you agree?" Next into the suitcase sailed a hair dryer, a cosmetics bag, two pairs of boots, and several pairs of shoes.

"I guess so," I conceded.

"He's ashamed of me, isn't he?" she said, jamming the suitcase closed. It was not a question I particularly wanted to answer.

"Aren't your dresses going to be all crunched up when you unpack at the other end?"

"They were all crunched up before I ever took them out of the closet," she said with a grin. "I imagine it's the kind of thing that makes Boris ashamed. But that's the way I am. Crazed! I just can't help myself." She threw her hands up in mock despair.

"So—I'm off to Lotus Land. Take care of Boris for me, not that he needs it. As a matter of fact, what he probably needs more than anything is a vacation from me. I hope he takes advantage of it—throws a few wild parties, invites all his friends over, has a swinging time. It'd be good for him."

"Boy," I said enviously, "I wish my mother had a little more of your attitude. It's funny: Boris is mad about *my* mother and I'm—" Suddenly I felt too self-conscious to say it. "—delighted we had a chance to talk," I finished lamely.

Sascha had a sort of disappointed look on her face. But taking her cue from me, she said politely, "I've enjoyed it, too, Annabel."

We shook hands, and then she picked up her suitcase and we walked to the front door.

I don't know what made me ask it—it must have been a premonition; but I said, "Do you have your ticket?"

"Oh my God, my ticket! I almost forgot." She rummaged through her purse. "I *did* forget. It's not in here and I've forgotten where I've put it. What did I do with it, where *is* it?!"

"Where did you see it last?" My mother always asks me that; sometimes it works.

"I can't remember ever seeing it. But I know I had a reservation."

"Then maybe it's at the reservation desk at the airport."

"Ai, of course! That's exactly where it is." She gave me a huge hug of gratitude.

"You know something, Sascha? You're *much* nicer than the maid said you were. That maid was a lousy judge of character."

She smiled at me wistfully. "I hope you're a better one."

Tuesday, April 23 – Friday, April 26

BORIS SAID THE OTB PLACE on 72nd Street was full of unshaven old bummy-looking men with racing sheets, unshaven middle-aged bummy-looking men with racing sheets, drunks, blacks, whites, Puerto Ricans—everybody poor and everybody standing around not talking to each other and looking as though they had no better place to be—even after they'd lost their last two dollars and had no more money to bet.

He said it was like a meeting place for the dregs of humanity—a club for creeps. They were so creepy-crawly he was afraid to ask any of them how to fill out the slip; so, in desperation, he finally asked the man at the window.

"I want to bet on Pace-o-Rama in the ninth at Roosevelt. How do I go about it?"

The man said, "How old are you, sonny?" and when Boris said nineteen, the man said, "Whaddya givin' me?" and threw him out.

He had to go to seven other OTBs before he found one that was too busy to notice his voice hadn't changed completely yet (or else they didn't care), and then guess where *that* was? The Port Authority Bus Terminal at 41st and Ninth. Hardly a convenient location. Boris was furious. Even though he came home with over a hundred dollars in his pocket, he was still furious when he got there.

"It's sickening! If I have to go to the Port Authority every day, I won't have time to do anything else. Tomorrow, I want *you* to go to the 72nd Street OTB and see if you make out any better."

"Me?" I squawked. "Why should I make out any better?"

"Because your voice won't give you away. Get dressed in your mother's clothes and go."

"Boris, I can't! I'd be terrified, don't ask me."

"I *am* asking you. That's all there is to it. Roger, over, and out."

Wednesday, April 24

So the next day, after I came home from school, I put on panty hose, my mother's black shoes with medium heels, a black silk dress of hers with a black cashmere sweater with mink on the collar, and lipstick, powder, rouge, eye shadow, and mascara.

On the way over to Broadway, three men tried to

pick me up. When I went to the window to place my bet (Bite the Bullet in the ninth at Belmont), the man said, "Scram, sweetheart. G'wan home and play with your dollies." So I went straight to the Port Authority—where five more men tried to pick me up and one nice man showed me how to fill out the slip—and came back with over a hundred dollars in my mother's pocketbook. I was furious, too—at Boris.

"That's enough of that! From now on, you do the betting, I'll do something else. Roger, over, and—"

"How're you going to do something else if you won't even wait for me to tell you what to do?"

"I've got to get out of these clothes before my mother comes home from Columbia. Just give me my assignment and make it snappy."

"I can't think that fast."

"Then beep me later. Beep me after the evening news and tell me what's going on tomorrow besides horses which I'm tired of the subject of. Roger, over, and out."

It turned out what he wanted me to do was meet the painter at his apartment the next day at five—he'd probably still be at the Port Authority but would get back as soon as he could. I should tell the painter to do whatever he thought necessary, regardless of cost, but he was to start immediately.

As far as news was concerned, there was going to be a strike at the Hunt's Point vegetable market; a gang of hoods would swipe a blind man's Seeing-Eye dog practically on the doorstep of the Lighthouse on 59th Street; the police would apprehend the alleged murderer in the Lenox Avenue holdup, thanks to the quick thinking of a young *Daily News* reporter, Bartholomew Bacon; the weather would be . . .

I told Boris to never mind the weather, clicked off, and called Bart.

"Hi-ya, Annie. How's my marshmallow?"

I giggled. "How's my Pulitzer Prize winner? Your story was terrific. Was the paper pleased?"

"Out of their skulls. So were the cops; because of my photo, they think they've got a lead on the guy who escaped."

"They'll get him within the next twenty-four hours."

"How do you know?"

"The same way I knew about Harry Steinberg, poor guy. Poor Belle. Anyway, if you don't believe me, watch Chris Borgen tomorrow night on CBS. There's a nice surprise in store for you—you're going to be a hero."

"No! Am I really?" He was delighted.

"Yes, really. Listen, Bart—do you want a human interest story? Hang around the Lighthouse on 59th, tomorrow—someone's going to swipe a blind man's Seeing-Eye dog. Can you use it?"

"Sure can. Does your ESP tell you when, though?

Maybe I could get there in time to prevent it."

"But then you wouldn't get your story."

"The heck with that. I'd rather save the guy's dog."

"That's generous and nice of you, Bart—but take it from me, you wouldn't be able to. The dog's already been stolen. I mean it's definitely going to be, although I don't know exactly when."

"I think I'll give it a whirl anyway. Want to come along?"

I was sorely tempted—but business before pleasure. I had to see the painter. Maybe another time, I told him, and said good-bye.

THURSDAY, APRIL 25

Julio María López, a tall, sad-eyed man with a face like a bloodhound, showed up on the dot of five. He lugubriously surveyed his immediate surroundings (hall, living room, and dining room), and pronounced them in very poor shape indeed.

"Very poor shape. Bad, terrible. How long since the last paint job? Don't tell me, I'll tell you." He picked off a piece of cracking paint by the front door, crumbled it in his fingers, and blew the dust out of his hand.

"Must be twenty years. Fifteen, anyway. Look at this here." He punched a bulging bubble of wall over the sideboard in the dining room and gloated with professional pride as three feet of dirty delft blue dropped to the floor. He patted the plaster underneath.

"Damp. Must've been you had a leak. Is the rest of the residence in the same condition?"

I showed him around. In each room, he pointed out something awful and made it worse—like the den, where he ripped off a whole strip of wallpaper to prove how many layers were underneath (five), and then ripped them all off, too. I decided he either knew the job was his or he was making sure it would be.

"Well, what do you think?" I asked after we'd completed the grand tour. "I mean, how much is it going to cost?"

He took out a pad and pencil and began estimating.

"Let's see what we got here: Nine rooms, fifteen closets, four baths, seven or eight walls in need of canvassing—if you don't canvas, your paint'll peel again in six months on account of your damp—seventeen window frames in need of burning and scraping. . . . I'd say, give or take a little, four ought to cover it."

"Four coats of paint? That much?"

"Four thousand dollars."

"I *thought* four coats of paint sounded like a lot—" Then it hit me. "FOUR THOUSAND DOLLARS! That's highway robbery!"

The painter didn't bat an eye. "It'll take three men a minimum of five days at union scale, and don't forget two coats of paint throughout. At today's prices, a good job like I'm going to do comes to five hundred bucks a room."

"How about skipping the closets?"

He didn't think much of that idea. "A saving of two hundred, merely. For the sake of two hundred you want to settle for dirty closets?"

I thought it was staggering, but Boris said regardless of cost. . . . So I told him to include the closets and start tomorrow. He said his men were on another job but he'd be there Monday with "three men 'n drop cloths." Then, he wanted to know what colors did I have in mind. White. All white, I told him. It seems there are a million shades of white: ivory white, cream white, white with a couple drops red, or with a couple drops brown—which did I want? *White* white, I told him. "Dead white? Okay, you're the boss. The usual finish—high gloss in the kitchen, semi on the woodwork, flat for the walls?" I told him high gloss all over—I liked things shiny. He said he'd give me anything I wanted—*he* didn't have to live there. Neither do I, I thought; and if Boris doesn't like my taste, he shouldn't have handed me the job in the first place.

Boris came home shortly after the painter had left, and I filled him in on the arrangements. He said he didn't care what color the place was, white, black, or burnt sienna, just as long as it got painted. The four-thousand-dollar tab didn't bother him either; he'd just won over four hundred on something called an Exacta and was giddy with power.

"When do they start?" was all he wanted to know.

"Jules said he and three men in drop cloths would come at eight on Monday. What's drop cloths—a new kind of coverall?"

"No, dummy. Drop cloths are what you drop over the furniture to protect it." He gazed at the living room in disgust. "Not that there's anything worth protecting. You know what we ought to do, Annabel? Get rid of the furniture before the painters start."

"All of it? That's a bit rash, don't you think?"

"Well, maybe not all of it, but a lot of it. It'll make the painters' work much easier. So you go downstairs now, and call the Salvation Army. Tell them to come tomorrow and to expect a full truckload. I'll stay here and tag what I want to throw out."

After a busy half hour on the phone I beeped Boris.

"What is it? I'm in the middle of the news, waiting for the sports to come on."

"The Salvation Army won't pick up 'til next week sometime. Goodwill Industries will pick up tomorrow but they've only got room for half a truckload. I called the super and asked if people were allowed to dump furniture on the street; he said you have to arrange it ahead with the Sanitation Department—sometimes weeks in advance and only on a pickup day, which tomorrow isn't. So what I want to know is this: Our housekeeper, Mattie, says her Granddaddy Clovis, who's deaf as a post and lives in a swamp in Georgia, just got burned out of his house. Is it all right if I give some of the stuff to her? Her brother could come for it tomorrow."

"I don't care what you do with it; just get it out of here before the weekend," he said impatiently. "It's your responsibility; you handle it."

"It's not my responsibility, it's your responsibility which you've bossily ordered me to assume. What am I getting out of this anyway? So far, it's been nothing but trouble and boring chores. When am I going to have some fun?"

"Saturday I'll take you shopping at Lord and Taylor. They're having a sale. We'll buy rugs, chairs, couches, lamps, and I'll let you buy a whole new wardrobe for Sascha, how's that?"

"That's more like it," I said, thinking of Sascha's closet full of crunched-up junk. I'd do anything for Sascha.

"Annabel, I know I've been bossy; but I'm so anxious to get it all together before my mother comes back, and there's so much to do."

One kind word and I melt like butter. "That's okay, Boris, I understand. It's just that we agreed that I'd help you use the Box to help your mother if you'd help *me* to use the Box to help other people. But lately, you haven't been keeping your end of the bargain."

"You're right," he admitted. "I've been so intent on the racing results, I haven't been on the lookout for your angle. But I will. I'll get on to something tomorrow, I promise."

FRIDAY, APRIL 26

At seven A.M. he called me. He was onto something.

"It's not much," he said apologetically, "but maybe it'll appeal to you. It's close by, too. There's a concert at the Mall this afternoon, and a little three-year-old kid called Gaylord gets separated from its mother. The mother finally shows up—that's the part I saw—but you might want to cruise the area and see if you can help the cops entertain the kid 'til the mother arrives."

"Boris, you're a prince. I'll try to be back in time for Operation Furniture Disposal."

"If you're not, don't worry. I'll manage."

Good old dependable Boris! When he says he'll be onto something, he's onto something.

Virginia was also onto something: What's-his-name's name! She'd heard it on the news and asked me at lunch if he was related to the Boston Bacons. I told her he was related to the Pittsburgh Bacons (who were distantly related to the Boston Bacons), and to please shut up before everybody at our table heard her.

So was my mother onto something: When I got home from school, she said Ape Face had been acting peculiarly lately. He spent most of his time in his room, listening to "Yellow Submarine."

"Sounds to me like he needs fresh air and exercise. Shall I take him to the park?" Mom thought that was a splendid suggestion.

On the way there, I told him to start playing some other record or he'd get caught with the Sony. He thanked me gratefully, and then asked if he could go to Boris's tomorrow to watch *The Phantom of the Opera* because on Sunday he had to go to a birthday party and would miss it. I told him sorry, but Boris and I were going to be out all day.

It wasn't a concert at the Mall; it was a concert at the Maul. People were pushing and shoving all over the lot; I didn't see how I was going to find one small kid in that mess. Actually, it was Ape Face who spotted him. He was sitting on the edge of the bandshell stage with his little overalled legs dangling down, and he was crying. A cop was hovering over him. I sat down next to him and said, "Aw, what's the matter? Lost your mommy, I'll bet."

"I didn't lose her; she lost me," he sobbed.

The cop turned to me in exasperation. "That's the only thing he's said for the last half hour—'I didn't lose her; she lost me.' I can't find out his name or his age or anything."

"He looks about three to me," I said. "Are you three?"

Gaylord stopped crying, nodded yes, and started crying again.

"You're doing better than I did," said the cop. "See what else you can find out."

"I know something," said Ape Face. "It's not a he, it's a she." A girl called Gaylord?

"You couldn't be more wrong," I said. "What makes you think so?"

"Short hair," said Ape Face. "A boy wouldn't have hair that short. Besides, it looks like a she." Gently, he prodded Gaylord's upper arm. "And it feels like a she. No muscles. It's a she."

"Okay, smarty, I'll ask. Are you a he or a she?"

"Yes," sobbed Gaylord.

"Maybe it doesn't know what it is," said the cop. At that, Gaylord stopped crying immediately.

"I do so. I'm a she."

"You're going great guns," said the cop admiringly. "See if you can find out her name."

It was an interesting challenge. I couldn't very well tell the cop I knew her name was Gaylord. Anyway, was it Somebody Gaylord, or Gaylord Somebody?

"What's your name?" I asked.

"My mommy lost me," said Gaylord.

"Crumb, we're back to that again," moaned the

cop.

Wait a minute! Maybe her name was Gail Ord.

"I bet I can *guess* your name," I said to her. "Just tell me what letter it begins with."

"She's too little to know that," said Ape Face.

"Your kid brother's a live one, isn't he," said the cop. "Why don't you let him do the guessing?"

"Joan," said Ape Face.

"Betsy," I said. I didn't want to guess it too quickly.

"Ellen," said Ape Face.

"Debbie."

"Sidney."

"Sidney! That's a boy's name," I said scornfully. Chalk one up for me.

"There's a girl in my class called Sidney."

"Grace," I said, ignoring him.

"Barbara," said Ape Face.

I was getting bored. "Gail!" I said triumphantly. "It's Gail, isn't it?" I studied her face for confirmation. There was none, although she did look a little puzzled.

"Something *like* Gail?" I asked. She nodded happily. Gailord, Gaylord—ah-ha!

"Gay!" I said.

"Gay," she acknowledged, and jumped into my lap.

"Hurray," said the cop.

"Shoot," said Ape Face. "I wanted to be the guesser."

"Can't win 'em all, Junior," said the cop.

"Gay's mommy lost Gay," said Gay, snuggling up

to me.

"But Gay's mommy is going to *find* Gay very soon, now. I have magic powers and I just know that."

"I wish I could say the same," grumbled the cop. "Else I got to drag her to the station house and stuff her with lollipops all afternoon."

"Mmn," said Gay. "Good."

There was a beep from the cop's walkie-talkie. "Officer Plonchik," he responded.

"Walt," squawked a voice, "This is Merve. I'm down by Bethesda Fountain. Walt, we got a lady here by the name of Lord who says she's lost her little girl."

"See, Gay. I told you I had magic powers. They found your mommy. Isn't that nice?"

Gay burst into tears.

"Jesus, Mary, and Joseph, *now* what's wrong?" said the cop.

"I don't want my mommy. I want lollipops."

"Can't win 'em all, Officer. Come on, Ape Face, let's get going."

I was back in time for the tail end of Operation Furniture Disposal. Apparently, between Mattie's brother and Goodwill Industries, it had been going quite smoothly, on the whole. I witnessed only one hairy moment—when one of the Goodwill men pointed to the Box and said to Boris, "You want we should take this also?"

"Don't you TOUCH that!" he said, screaming like a banshee.

They must have thought he was nuts.

Saturday, April 27

LORD AND TAYLOR WAS A TRIP and a half! Between ten thirty and one, under the solicitous guidance of a Mr. Hemphill, Boris bought: three rugs, two sofas, one love seat, one coffee table, one dining-room table, ten feet of sectional bookcases, six lamps, a digital clock, and an enormous desk for Sascha's workroom; all of it modern, and—as the conscientious Mr. Hemphill felt obliged to remind us—all of it on sale.

"You're quite sure about this merchandise, are you? Because it's nonreturnable, you know."

"Perfectly all right with me," said Boris, his eyes glistening with enthusiasm. "There's nothing I like more than a good bargain."

Mr. Hemphill wrote up the order and promised delivery within five days, which he said was only possible because the items we had purchased were floor samples and the department store wanted to clear out the old inventory to make way for the new. Boris couldn't have cared less what the reason was, as long as he got the stuff before Sascha came home.

"Now, it's your turn," he said amiably. "Let's see what's on sale in the way of clothes. You're about the same size as Sascha; you can even try everything on, if you like."

"What I'd like is lunch," I protested. "I'm too weak to stand up."

Boris fished a lint-covered Life Saver out of his pocket. "Here, eat this. It's quick sugar. If I'm going to get to OTB, we won't have time for lunch."

So from one 'til four, under the solicitous guidance of a Miss Fickett, I bought: two coats, six dresses, five pairs of slacks, one "very lovely gown, ideal for entertaining in the home," and one mink jacket, marked down from seventy-five hundred to a mere two thousand. It was too good to be true!

"What's wrong with it?" I asked suspiciously.

"Not a thing," said Miss Fickett. "It's a superb wrap and a wonderful bargain." So we bought that, too.

Somewhere in the dim recesses of my brain lurks the memory of my father gently chiding my mother for spending two hundred dollars at a January white sale. "A bargain is no bargain if you can't afford it in the first place" is what he said. He said a mouthful.

That night, when Boris and I added up what we'd blown at Lord and Taylor, it came to a grand total of eighty-three hundred and some odd dollars.

"Goodness," said Boris mildly. "That's quite a tab, isn't it?" The tone of his voice was calm enough, but he gave himself away by twiddling a pencil between his upper and lower teeth. He never clickety-clicks like that unless there's something heavy on his mind.

"Quite a tab is right. It's absolutely horrendous. Between eighty-five hundred today and four thousand to the painter, you're in hock for over twelve thousand."

"I can add," he said.

"How much money have you made so far?"

"About two thousand. So I'm actually only in hock for ten, not twelve. And I would have had almost six hundred more—but I couldn't get to OTB yesterday because I had to stay home and supervise the furniture disposal. I'd been counting on you to do that, but I knew how much your good deed meant to you." That's what I call zinging it in. "I hope it was worth it," he added.

On the theory that he'd only feel worse if I told him he'd sacrified almost six hundred dollars for the sake of Gay Lord and her lollipops, I decided to dress the story up a little.

"Wow, was it worth it! When I found that kid, she was crying so hysterically, she was on the verge of convulsions. I left her wreathed in smiles."

"You feel good, huh?" I felt rotten.

"Oh yes. It was a heartwarming experience."

He sighed. "Then it was worth it." I felt rottener.

"Boris, don't you think maybe you should call off the painter?"

"What—and have Sascha come home to brand-new furniture in the old slum surroundings, with musty old closets full of brand-new clothes? That'd be about as effective as I don't know what—hanging a silk purse on a sow's ear." He blinked at himself. "Well anyway, you know what I mean.

"No," he said, "I'll go ahead with the painter. If she doesn't come back too soon, I think I can make it. But from now on, I can't afford to miss a day of OTB."

"You also can't afford to spend another dime until you've made ten thousand dollars."

Clickety-click.

"Now what are you thinking?" I asked.

"About the new washer, dryer, stove, fridge, and dishwasher."

"Forget it. They'll have to wait."

"That's just it. They can't."

"Boris, you've gone around the bend! Why can't they?"

Sheepishly, he said, "Because yesterday, I gave the old ones to Mattie's brother. By now, they're on their way to Granddaddy Clovis's Georgia swamp."

"Dear God in heaven! You mean there's nothing in the kitchen but one-two-three-four-*five gaping holes*?

Aside from everything else, how do you expect to live? What are you going to wear? What are you going to eat?"

"Life Savers, tuna fish, dried apricots. I'll manage. It's only 'til Monday."

"Monday." I stared stupidly at him.

"Monday the new stuff is coming. I bought it early this morning from a discount store on Broadway—for fifteen hundred."

"On sale, I suppose."

"Of course, on sale. It's not as though I'd want to return it—it's indispensable equipment. The five gaping holes, as you so picturesquely described them, have to be filled up with something."

"Boris, it's nitty-gritty time. How are you going to get that money before your mother comes back, and when *is* she coming back?"

"Well, let's see. She left Monday the 22nd, and said she'd be gone two weeks. Which would mean she'd be back on—uh . . . thirty days hath September, April, June, and November—she'd be back on Monday, May 6th. Except she's never yet been back when she's said she would—she's always at least a week late. So assuming she follows her usual pattern, that would give me—today's the 27th—that would give me twelve working days at just under six hundred a day which comes to—"

"Only just under seventy-two hundred dollars."

"Congratulations on learning your twelves tables."

"Don't change the subject, Boris. Seventy-two hundred dollars is not enough. What are you going to do?"

After an interminable period of clicking, his face lit up.

"There *is* something I can do. I can't win more than six hundred a day in any one *place;* but what's to stop me from going to two places a day? I could go to . . ." He snapped his fingers impatiently. "Think of another big OTB parlor where they won't notice my age."

"Penn Station? Grand Central?"

"Penn Station! Perfect! It's almost around the corner from the Port Authority. Don't worry about a thing—I've got it made! A billion for Boris coming right up!"

From that point on, things really began to move. In fact, the events were so numerous and happened so much on top of each other, I can hardly keep them straight. But I'll try.

Sunday, April 28 – Thursday, May 2

Boris beeped me early; he was onto something for me: Bob Dylan was going to make a surprise appearance this afternoon in Sheep Meadow. Did I know somebody who could benefit from that advance information? "Can't you?" I asked him. He said he had to spend the day putting away knickknacky ornaments before the painters came on Monday.

So I called Bart (maybe he could get an exclusive interview); and I called my friend Leslie, who adores Bob Dylan, and gave her a strong hint. (P.S. The next day in school, she told me all about it. Bob Dylan had been wonderful, but her purse got ripped off. So much for *that* good deed.)

Boris won fifty dollars betting on a ball game with Harvey Kuchel. I was very angry with him and told him he was a rat fink. He agreed—said it was just that he couldn't bear to have a day go by without earning something—and promised never to do it again. At least he was honest with me.

Monday, April 29

Boris beeped me before breakfast with a list of murder, arson, rape, and robbery as long as your arm. (Good for Bart, but a little too gory for my taste.) And a spectacular item for me: Loretta Burke, daughter of Mr. and Mrs. John Burke of Manhattan, thought to have been abducted from her dormitory room at C. W. Post College over six months ago and presumed dead, turned up safe and sound in Burlington, Vermont with her boyfriend. According to the Burlington chief of police, it was a case of "*se*duction not *ab*duction." Very droll fellows, those Vermonters.

I called Bart before I left for school, gave him my ESP predictions for the day and learned, much to his gratification and mine, that his interview with Dylan would appear in next Sunday's magazine section, *with by-line.*

And when I got home from school, I called the Burkes. Do you know how many John Burkes there are in the Manhattan phone book? Eighteen. ("Hello, are you the Burkes with the missing daughter? No? Sorry, wrong Burkes, good-bye.")

When I finally located the right ones, and convinced them of the joyful news about Loretta in

Vermont, Mrs. Burke said, "You better be wrong. Because if she did a thing like that to us, I don't ever want to see her again, do you, John?" And Mr. Burke said, "If she did a thing like that to us, I'd better never see her again because if I do, I'll wring her neck with my bare hands."

"Oh dear," I said, and hung up.

The only good deed I could have salvaged out of that situation would have been to find Loretta and warn her to stay in Vermont. Unfortunately, I didn't know how to do that.

Boris reported in, late that night.

"Boris the Billionaire speaking. My two-a-day plan worked brilliantly. I won eleven hundred and fifty-three dollars and twenty-four cents. How did you make out?"

"Only so-so. Listen, I can't talk. I'm in the middle of studying. We're having a monster bio quiz tomorrow."

"Don't bother. Save yourself the trouble. There's going to be a wildcat strike of school-building maintenance men; the schools'll all be closed. See? I did a good deed for *you* for a change."

"Super! What else is new?"

"The kitchen equipment is all in; and the painters have absolutely gutted the apartment. It looks like Pompeii. I hope they get through with this preparatory stage soon; I'm choking to death in the plaster."

"Poor Boris." I clucked sympathetically. "Just keep reminding yourself: It's all in a good cause."

"Right. Speaking of good causes, would you know how I could line up a psychiatrist for Sascha for when she comes home? A new environment is only half the battle; she needs other kinds of help as well."

"Offhand, I can't think of any. Besides, even if I could, how do you know you can persuade her to go?"

"I don't. But I'd like to have a name or two up my sleeve, just in case I catch her in a receptive frame of mind some day."

I told him I'd do my best, and said good-bye. Then I put away my bio book and sat up half the night, rereading *Gone With The Wind.*

Tuesday, April 30

At seven thirty, Ma woke me. "Up, up, up, Annabel—you'll be late! What did you do, forget to set the alarm?"

"No school," I mumbled, and buried my face in the pillow.

"Nobody skips school in this house unless they're sick," she said firmly. "Now get up." She yanked the covers off me.

"There isn't any school," I said, yanking them back. "Something about a maintenance men's strike."

"Oh that," she said. "I just heard that on the news.

It only applies to public schools. Your school is open and you're going to it."

"Meanie!" I said.

"Grouchy!" said Ma, and laughed.

She won't laugh when she sees my report card. I walked into bio totally unprepared and flunked the test cold. So much for *Boris's* good deed.

On the stairwell between classes, Virginia asked me how Bart was. I told her he was fine, why? She said that on Sunday she and James had had a frightful row—it was all over between them—so she was wondering if I'd mind if she invited Boris to the class dance. (!!!) I told her I'd mind very much because it was all over between me and Bart, too—I'd decided it was Boris I really loved—and *I* was going to invite him to the class dance.

At ten thirty that night, Boris beeped me, terribly upset.

"The Box isn't working! It's on, but there's nothing on the screen except grainy snow and a lot of staticky noise. It's as though all the channels were off the air."

"That's very odd," I said.

"It's worse than odd; it's a potential disaster. What if the Box is permanently on the blink? I'll be finished. Ruined!"

I told him not to panic; I'd get Ape Face up there first thing in the morning—maybe he could fix it.

At five after eleven, Boris beeped again.

"Never mind Ape Face. It's working now," he said somberly.

"But that's great," I said. "What are you so gloomy about?"

"Because I've just found out why it wasn't working before. Tomorrow there's going to be a total blackout in New York and Westchester, from five fourteen in the afternoon 'til eleven at night. Which means that not only did I miss today's OTB results because all the channels were off the air tomorrow, but I am also going to miss tomorrow's OTB results for Thursday because there won't be any electricity."

"Gee, that is a setback, isn't it? But you made something today, didn't you?"

"Eleven hundred and ninety dollars and forty-three cents. Still, I'm way behind schedule."

"What a shame you can't drag the Box to New Jersey and plug it in there. But I suppose that's not too practical a suggestion, is it?"

"Not too," he said witheringly. "Try again."

"Well . . . for the rest of the week, beginning Thursday, why don't you go to three OTB places? Port Authority, Penn Station, *and* Grand Central. That ought to do it."

"If I don't drop dead of exhaustion. Roger, over, and pray for me."

Wednesday, May 1

Before breakfast, I called Bart.

"What's the bad news for today, Annie old girl?" When I told him, he sounded rather disappointed.

"A blackout? That's all?"

"Isn't that enough?"

"It's all right, I guess, but it doesn't give me an advantage over any of the other reporters on the paper. We'll all be in the same boat—except that they'll be stumbling around in the dark and I'll be stumbling around in the dark with a flashlight."

"Bartholomew Bacon, you are becoming entirely too dependent on my ESP. See what you can do on your own, for once. Take your flashlight to the New York Foundling Hospital and entertain frightened children with hand shadows on the wall. That'd make a nice story. Or guide hysterical office workers out of the subway."

Subway! I suddenly realized that Dad always took the subway home. He'd be trapped himself!

"Anyway, Bart, my ESP tells me breakfast is getting cold. Good-bye."

Another good deed coming up!

"Dad, you're not eating eggs again, are you?"

"Why not? I love eggs."

"But they're full of cholesterol, and at your age . . . Dad, do you know the statistics on the number of men in their forties who drop dead of heart attacks? It's perfectly alarming. And the kind of men it happens to are men just like you: Men in your socioeconomic bracket, under a constant strain from high-pressure desk jobs, who don't get enough exercise."

I stared fixedly at his stomach. "I don't like to say this, Dad, but you're getting flabby in the gut. You should get more exercise, shouldn't he, Ma?"

"He probably should, darling, but it's difficult, living in New York."

"He could walk home from work. Walking is wonderful exercise. Dad, why don't you walk home from work, starting tonight."

"I wouldn't dream of it," said Dad.

"Well, then," I intoned darkly, "don't blame me if you keel over at your desk some day. I just hope you have plenty of insurance to provide for your widow and your poor, fatherless, uneducated children."

"When is it going to happen?" asked Ape Face, his chin beginning to quiver.

"Now look what you've done!" whispered Ma angrily. She threw her napkin on the table and went over to comfort him.

"It's not, Ben, it's not." To me, she said, "Annabel, what is this morbid preoccupation with your father's death? It's very neurotic of you."

I decided to try to kill two birds with one stone.

"It isn't neurotic, Ma. Besides, if it were, I bet you

wouldn't even know a good psychiatrist to send me to." Dad and Ma exchanged concerned glances.

"No, I don't. I'm happy to say no one in this family has ever needed one . . . so far." She looked at her watch. "Shake a leg, Annabel, or you and Ben will be late."

When I came home from school, I raced to the Japanese store to buy some fat candles for the apartment. (If Dad was going to be trapped in the subway, I could at least make the waiting a little brighter for Mom.) The Japanese store was fresh out of candles.

As predicted by Boris, the lights came back on at eleven. Dad slammed in the door half an hour later in a foul temper.

"Poor Bill," said Ma, oozing with empathy. "Was the subway a nightmare?"

"I wouldn't know," he said. "From what I hear, most people managed to get out of the subway fairly quickly—but I wasn't in it."

"Then where were you?" she said. "What happened to you?"

"What happened to me was I listened to *her,*" he said, jerking his head venomously in my direction. "I got to thinking about what she'd said about exercise, and made up my mind to leave the office a little early and walk home. I have just spent the last six hours in a stalled elevator with a lot of overwrought office workers and Luther Parkhurst whom I loathe. Comparatively speaking, the subway would have been a festival of fun."

I was seized with an uncontrollable fit of giggling.

"For someone who displayed such filial concern for me this morning, you seem to be displaying an astonishing lack of it, now," Dad roared. "What's so funny about my being stuck in an elevator?"

"I can't explain."

"Then go to your room!"

BEEP, BEEP, BEEP. "Boris," I chortled. "You'll never guess what I've done!" I filled him in, and ended by saying, "The whole day was a total loss!"

"Mine wasn't," said Boris. "The painters are almost finished—they'll definitely be through by Friday, Lord and Taylor called to say they're definitely delivering the stuff Friday, and best of all, I made two hundred dollars."

"How did you manage that?"

"I bought out all the candles in the Japanese store and sold them to people in the building for two dollars apiece."

"You might have saved one for my mother," I said, and collapsed laughing all over again.

When I'd calmed down, I asked him what was on the Box for tomorrow. He said he hadn't bothered to watch since he'd missed the OTB results anyway; but he had listened to the radio and heard something sort of baffling. Apparently, during the blackout, burglars had made a clean sweep of the ground floor of Tiffany's—over two million dollars worth of precious gems. The police said it was almost as though the men who did it had known in advance that the burglar alarms would be inoperative. Didn't I think that was curious? Very curious indeed, I told him, and clicked off.

When Mom and Dad were safely asleep, I crept to the kitchen and called Bart.

"You know what my ESP tells me now?" I asked.

"Wha—?" he said drowsily.

"That you're a common thief!" Instantly awake, he demanded to know what I was talking about. The Tiffany robbery, I told him.

"I swear to you, Annie, on my mother's grave, I had nothing to do with it."

"Well, somebody knew—and knew in advance. *I* didn't tell anyone except you. Did *you* tell someone?"

"Only my neighbor, Mrs. Krasny. I didn't want her to be all alone in the dark in that crummy building of ours, so I gave her a flashlight and told her I'd heard that Con Ed was having trouble with Big Allis; that in all probability there would be a blackout later on in the day. She thanked me very kindly for the information."

"I'll bet she did. Bart, far be it from me to tell you how to further your own career, but if I were you, I'd investigate Mrs. Krasny."

"Is that what your ESP tells you?"

"No, that's what my common sense tells me."

THURSDAY, MAY 2

The next morning, the paper was full of it. Bart and the police must have worked fast because the last edition of the *Daily News* goes to press at two thirty A.M.

> As the result of a tip from one of our own *Daily News* reporters, Bartholomew Bacon, police last night were able to recover an estimated two million dollars worth of Tiffany jewels, stolen during yesterday's blackout. The cache was found intact in the West 52nd Street apartment of Mrs. Helen Krasny, long-time girlfriend of gang leader Salvio (Lean Julian) Vizzini, and neighbor of Mr. Bacon. When apprehended, Mrs. Krasny spat at Bacon (see photo), and said, "Fine neighbor you turned out to be. Lean Julian'll get you for this!"

And to think I rang that woman's doorbell!

Since the gods seemed to be on my team, I thought I'd take another whack at finding a shrink for Sascha. In my free study period, I paid a call on the school psychologist, Dr. Vera Artunian.

"Dr. Artunian?" I said, peeking into her office.

She looked up, removed her reading glasses, and said, "It's Annabel Andrews, isn't it? Come in, my dear, come in. And close the door. We don't want the whole school to hear, do we?" She gestured toward a big leather chair opposite her desk. I sat down.

"Now," she said, "tell me what's on your mind. You have a little problem of some sort?"

"It's not my problem, it's my friend's problem. My friend, you see, has this mother . . ."

"Yes?" she said encouragingly.

"And the mother is crazy. Very nice—but irresponsible and crazy. Plumb nuts. She makes my friend very unhappy."

"I'm sorry to hear that." Artunian gazed at me thoughtfully and then, ever so casually, said, "Tell me more about your mother."

"*My* mother!" I gasped. "I'm not talking about *my* mother, I'm talking about my *friend's* mother."

In a warm and confiding tone, she said, "Annabel, when we have feelings that are difficult to express, we often find it easier to ascribe those feelings to someone other than ourselves. I can't tell you the number of patients who come to talk to me about a 'friend.'"

"But . . ." I began.

"But," she continued with a fanatical gleam in her eye, "it's such a transparent maneuver! I assure you, you can't fool me—although you *can* trust me."

"Dr. Artunian, I think you're crazier than my

friend's mother," I said, and fled from her office. The gods weren't on my team after all.

At home, Boris was having his own troubles.

"Listen," he said over the walkie-talkie, "I've just had a near miss. A short while ago, I came across one of the painters sprawled all over my room, watching the Box."

"Wow—that's dangerous! Do you think he caught on? What was he watching?"

"Only a game show, fortunately; but we've got to move that set to a safer place. I wouldn't want to take a chance on it happening again. Let's move it back down to the Ape's room."

I could see there was no point in arguing. "Okay," I sighed, "but you carry it."

At the sight of the Box, Ape Face was, at first, thoroughly bewildered. "But I like my Sony very much. You don't want to trade again, do you?"

When Boris assured him he didn't, he was delighted. "Great! Tomorrow I can watch *Torture Garden,* which I was going to have to miss on Saturday."

"Oh, no you don't, kiddo," snarled Boris. "That Box is still my property and don't you dare lay a hand on it. If your mother sees that it's working, the jig is up."

"Is someone taking my name in vain?" asked Ma, poking her head in the door. "Oh horrors, what's that great, hulking, no-good thing doing here again, Ben?

I thought you gave it back to Boris because you were tired of tinkering with it."

"But then you began to miss it, didn't you, Ben?" prompted Boris. Ape Face nodded.

"Ma," I whispered, "you said you'd been worried about him. Let him keep it—it's good therapy for him."

"All right," said Ma. "I just wish it didn't take up so much space. I keep barking my shins on it."

When she left, Boris said, "Don't forget, Ape, you're not to touch it. If you want to watch television, play the Sony."

"And another thing not to forget," I added, "is when you're watching the Sony, don't play 'Yellow Submarine,' play something else."

For the rest of the evening, all I heard coming out of his room was "Lucy in the Sky with Diamonds." My brother is a very literal-minded kid.

Friday, May 3

IN RETROSPECT, I find it hard to believe that so many grisly things could have happened in one twenty-four hour period. But they did.

When I got home from school, Hector said, "Are you going to be seeing your upstairs amigo?"

"I guess so; why?"

"Because this came for him." A telegram. "Shall I deliver it or if you're going to be seeing him, you can give it to him yourself."

"I'll give it to him," I said, stuffing it into my pocket. "Would you take me up there now, por favor?"

I rang the bell. (Boris, unlike Sascha, always keeps the door locked.) He let me in promptly, and with great pride showed me around the apartment. To describe it as dazzling would have been a gross understatement; in the high gloss *white* white, you could practically see your own reflection.

"Boris, it's ravishing!" I exclaimed. "But empty. Where's the furniture?"

"I'm waiting for it now. It'll be coming any minute."

"Speaking of coming," I produced the telegram, "this came for you. What do you suppose it is?"

He stared at it the way you'd stare at a hooded cobra—with fear and loathing.

"Nothing good," he croaked. "You open it. I'm afraid to look."

I ripped open the envelope, read the message—and felt the blood congealing in my veins. From my lips to the tips of my toes, I was numb all over.

I wanted to break it to him gently. "Boris," I whispered, "it's very bad."

"It's Sascha, isn't it? She's dead."

"Worse."

"What could be worse?"

"She's coming back—*soon.*"

"That's definitely worse." He clutched his head. "How soon?"

I didn't have the guts to tell him. Wordlessly, I held out the telegram. He took it with trembling fingers.

" 'Home for Derby Day or before. Love Sascha.' Derby Day," he repeated dully. "My head doesn't seem to be functioning. When is it? *What* is it?"

"The Kentucky Derby. It's tomorrow."

Boris collapsed against the wall like Raggedy Andy and closed his eyes.

I grabbed him by the shoulders and shook him 'til he opened them again.

"Boris!" I shouted, "This is no time to go into a catatonic state! Your mother is coming home tomorrow or maybe even today. You've got to *do* something!"

"It's no use," he said faintly. "It's too late."

"It's *not* too late!" I said, punching him on the shoulder. "Pull yourself together and DO something!"

"All right, Annabel. Tell me what to do. Just tell me what to do and I'll do it."

"That's the spirit." Boris's mind may have been out to lunch, but mine was clicking along like an IBM computer. "First, how much money do you have?"

"Four thousand three hundred and forty-three dollars and sixty-seven cents. And I owe . . ."

"Never mind what you owe. You're going to take that money right now to OTB and bet it all on the Kentucky Derby."

"How can I? I don't know which horse."

I looked at my watch. "The race'll be starting in twenty minutes. By the time you've gotten to the Port Authority, I'll have seen the results on the Box, downstairs. Call me as soon as you get there and I'll tell you which horse."

"But suppose the furniture comes while you're downstairs? Who's going to sign for the furniture?"

"Aargh," I groaned. "Boris, you're the bleeding limit! Get your coat and your money. I'll run down and tell Ape Face to watch the Box. When you get to Port Authority, you can call *him.* I'll wait here for the furniture."

"All right," he said. Putty in my hands, thank goodness.

I ran downstairs, gave Ape Face his instructions, made him repeat them to me twice to make sure he understood, and ran back up to Boris's.

"All set," I panted. "Now, GO! When that horse comes in first tomorrow, you'll make a fortune which, on Monday, you can deposit in Sascha's savings account. She'll never know the difference."

"I'll have to pay a huge income tax."

"Which is better? To pay a huge income tax on a huge amount of money, or be in *hock* for a huge amount of money? Don't be stupid. Now, get out of here!" I pushed him out the door.

Boris had no sooner left when Lord and Taylor arrived. Clothes first, I decided. I pushed all of Sascha's old, crummy stuff to the back of the closet and lovingly hung up the new collection in the front. The mink I hung in the hall closet where it put the other coats to shame.

Now for the furniture. After a few minutes of back-breaking (and fruitless) shoving and lugging, I realized I couldn't possibly manage it alone. Would Hector be willing to help me? For a slight fee, he would—and did.

"Gracias," I said when we were finished.

"De nada," he said. Five dollars of my own allowance was not what I called de nada—but oh, well, what can you do?

At five o'clock, having shifted from his catatonic mood to a manic one, Boris bounded in the door.

"It's Ticker Tape by half a length. I'm going to be rich, *rich*, RICH!" he hollered.

"How do you like where I put the furniture?" I asked.

"Perfection. Everything is perfection. *You* are perfection!" he said, swinging his jacket in circles over his head. "Let's sit on the new sofa and plan how we're going to spend all the leftover money."

The phone rang.

"Let's answer the phone, first."

"You answer it," he said nervously.

"Boy, Boris, I have to read your telegrams, answer your phones—what are you, chicken or something?"

"Yes," he said. "I'm so afraid our luck will run out."

I picked up the phone, listened for a moment, hung up, and said, "I think it just has. That was my mother. She sounds like a blast of wind from the North Pole and wants me to come home 'this instant.' "

"I'll come with you," said Boris manfully. "Just as long as it has to do with your mother; I'm not quite ready for my own, yet."

I don't think he could have been ready for mine,

either. I know I wasn't. She was standing at the front door, waiting to pounce like a panther when I came in.

"Annabel Andrews," she said, ignoring Boris altogether. "You knew all about that set of Ben's, didn't you!"

Boris and I looked at each other and exchanged simultaneous telepathic messages: Which set is she talking about? Boris shook his head a millimeter of an inch. Don't ask that—you'll give it away, he was saying.

"You deliberately encouraged that child to do something he knew was strictly against my wishes."

"I didn't encourage him, Ma, I just didn't *dis*courage him." That seemed noncommittal enough.

"As a responsible older sister, you *should* have."

"I'm sorry," I mumbled.

"Don't apologize to me—apologize to him. I've had to tell him he can't watch any television at all for a month."

Like two beaten dogs, Boris and I slunk down the hall to the Ape's room. "Our luck's running out. I knew it," muttered Boris.

"Think positive," I muttered back. "Maybe she only found the Sony."

Crossing our fingers, we opened the door and went in. The Ape was sitting cross-legged on the floor in the very spot where the Box had been.

"Hi," he said dejectedly.

"Hi," we said. I sat down on the bed. Boris closed

the door and sat down next to me.

After casting a furtive glance behind him to make sure the door was really closed, Ape Face began burrowing feverishly in the toy chest. Like a mole, flipping pieces of multicolored Lego over his shoulder, he dug down to the bottom and came up with his precious Sony.

"For you," he said to Boris.

"Thanks, Ape, but you keep it. It's no good to me anyhow."

"Why not? It works great."

To me, Boris said, "Your brother doesn't seem to understand the significance of the Box."

"I don't think he ever did," I answered. "Ape Face, Boris appreciates the gesture, but he doesn't want your Sony. Put it away now, before Mom catches you."

With a vast sigh of relief, Ape Face replaced it in its bed of Lego.

"Say, Ape, when your mother took the Box away, do you know what she did with it?" That hadn't occurred to me. Maybe it was still in the back hall and we could reclaim it, secretly. Hope springs eternal!

"She gave it away." Hope, schmope.

The thought of somebody else benefiting from his Box was almost more than Boris could bear.

"Ugh," he groaned. "Who to?"

"To Mattie—for Granddaddy Clovis. Mattie said he was deaf as a post and wouldn't get much use out of the sound part, but he sure would enjoy looking at the pictures."

"At least it's not in the hands of an unscrupulous person," I pointed out.

"Yeah," said Boris. "Small comfort, though."

"I feel so bad," said Ape Face.

"Don't," said Boris. "We're the ones who made you watch the Derby."

"But that isn't when it happened," said Ape Face. Poor, guileless cretin.

Boris rose slowly to his feet. "Just what do you mean?" he asked.

"It happened after that. As soon as I saw it was Ticker Tape . . ." he got a glimpse of Boris's face and hesitated.

"Go on," said Boris. He looked like Jack the Ripper. Ape Face wiggled nearer to me.

"I switched to *Torture Garden.* And then the phone rang and I knew it would be you; so I left the room in a hurry and forgot to turn the set off and-that's-how-she-caught-me," he finished.

"That . . . is . . . exactly . . . what . . . I . . . told . . . you . . . never . . . to . . . do, isn't it?" said Boris.

Then he did something I would never have thought him capable of. Repeating, "Isn't that what I told you never to do, *isn't it*?" he shook Ape Face back and forth 'til I thought his teeth would fall out.

Next it was my turn to do something I never would

have thought *I'd* be capable of. I hauled off and socked Boris in the chops—hard.

Then all three of us stood around—dumbstruck and miserable.

Finally, Ape Face said in tones of great awe, "Gee, Annabel, you're as tough as John Wayne!"

"I had it coming to me," said Boris, licking his swollen lip.

"And you *sound* like John Wayne," said Ape Face.

Boris and I looked at each other and grinned. Then I reached out and touched his cheek. Then he reached out and stroked the Ape's hair.

"Peace all around?" he asked.

"Peace," said my brother and I.

Saturday morning, May 4

I WAS UPSTAIRS AT BORIS'S, helping him put the finishing touches on the apartment. He was vacuuming and I was placing bunches of forsythia and pussy willows around the living room. We were in no particular hurry because unless Sascha had taken the Red Eye Express (which would have gotten her in early in the morning), she wouldn't be arriving 'til mid afternoon, at least. I felt strangely lighthearted.

"You know something, Boris?"

"What?" he shouted, over the roar of the Hoover.

"I feel as if a great load has been taken off my mind."

Boris turned off the Hoover. "You feel as if what?"

"As if a great load has been taken off my mind."

"How so?"

"Well—this may shock you, but I think I'm glad we don't have the Box anymore."

"Speak for yourself, John," he said glumly.

"Boris, how much money are you going to win on Ticker Tape?"

"I don't know exactly, but a lot. Around fifty thou, I guess."

"Right. So you've accomplished your mission, haven't you? The apartment is looking lovely, Sascha has a new wardrobe, and with the rest of the money, you'll be able to take care of the school bill, the back taxes, the housekeeper, the accountant, the psychiatrist—incidentally, I haven't gotten a lead on one, yet, but I'll keep trying."

"Please do," he said. "That's terribly important. Unless there's a fundamental change in her personality, all of this," he waved his arm at the living room, "won't amount to a hill of beans. Within a year, everything new will look old and cruddy again, and we'll be back in debt."

"*But*—on the assumption that a) I will find her a psychiatrist and b) you will persuade her to go to him (or her), you *have* accomplished your mission, have you not?"

"I guess so. Still . . ."

"Still what?"

"I still wish I had the Box."

"What for? So you can make more and more and more money? That's piggy of you. You don't *need* more money; and since money was the only thing you used the Box for, you no longer need the Box."

"I guess not," he reluctantly admitted. "But what about you? Aren't you going to miss it? You liked knowing about the future, didn't you?"

"No," I said slowly. "I think, actually, I hated it. To know about hijackings and fires and murders," I thought about Belle Steinberg, "and know people are going to suffer from things you can't prevent—that's not fun. It's very depressing."

"What about the things you could prevent, what about the good deeds? Playing gin rummy with your little, old, frail grandmother so she wouldn't get caught in the blizzard."

"Boris, I could spend the rest of my life doing things like that—but out of all the millions of opportunities that would present themselves, I'd be constantly having to decide which little old lady to save. I don't want that responsibility and I'm glad I don't have it.

"Furthermore, good deeds involve a great deal of work and aren't all that easy to do. Take my father, for example. I managed to keep him out of the subway, so what happened? He got stuck in an elevator instead.

"Come to think of it, all my good deeds were a complete washout—with one exception.. . ." Bart. But I had never told Boris about Bart and didn't plan to now, or ever.

"The little kid in the park?"

"Yes. That's the one I mean."

What *about* Bart? I suddenly thought. No more ESP for him! I'd better warn him.

"Boris, I have an errand to do. I'll be back in an hour, okay?"

"Sure. Take your time. While you're gone, I'll Windex the glass coffee table—it's covered with fingerprints."

In the lunchroom next door to the *Daily News*, while waiting for Bart, I prepared my pep talk to him. In fact, I prepared a whole scenario, which went roughly like this:

BART
[enthusiastically]
Hello. I came as soon as I could. Have you been waiting long?

ANNIE
No, no. Only a couple of minutes. How's everything going?

BART
So great, it's out of sight! You read Thursday's paper, didn't you? I'm a hero to the police department, a hero to my paper. By Sunday, I'll have my own by-line, and by the end of the week, I'll probably have a raise. And I owe it all to you. [*He clasps Annie's hands in gratitude.*]

ANNIE

[modestly]

Nonsense! That's a ridiculous thing to say.

BART

Where would I be today without you and your ESP, tell me that, huh?

ANNIE

[earnestly and with conviction]

Bart, I may have given you a few hot tips, but I didn't write your articles for you. You're a fine, fine writer. A talented writer. You do believe that about yourself, don't you?

BART

[smiling shyly]

I'm beginning to, I guess.

ANNIE

That's what I like to hear. You've got to develop more self-confidence. Because I know you have a fantastic future ahead of you.

BART

Tell me about it. Do I get the Pulitzer Prize?

ANNIE

[fiddles with silverware, takes long drink of chocolate float, averts eyes]

I don't know.

BART

[agitatedly]

How can you not know?! What does your ESP tell you?

ANNIE

That's the thing of it, Bart; it doesn't. You see— [*She grips his hand to give him courage.*] I don't have my ESP anymore. I've lost it.

BART

[disbelieving]

You mean it's *gone*?! Just like [*snaps fingers*] that, it's gone? Are you sure?

ANNIE

[shakes head sadly]

I'm afraid so. From now on, you'll have to go it alone without my help.

BART

[dismayed out of his skull]

Oh no!

ANNIE

Just have confidence, and you'll be fine. I'm sure you will. Someday. [*She rises, slips on gloves, gracefully extends hand.*] I'll probably read all about you winning that Pulitzer Prize, and I'll think to myself, "I knew him, once." [*She presses her gloved hand to his cheek.*]

BART

You mean I'm never going to see you again? You mean this is—[*He chokes on the word. She says it for him.*]

ANNIE

Good-bye.

"What about hello, first?" said Bart.

I jumped a mile high in the air. Bart was sitting across the table from me.

"How long have you been there?" I asked.

"For about five minutes. I didn't want to interrupt your reverie."

"Was I talking aloud all that time?" How embarrassing!

"No, good-bye was all I heard." Whew!

"Say, Bart, have they caught Lean Julian yet?"

"This morning. I wish you'd told me yesterday. I could have been there and it would have made a fitting climax to the story."

I mumbled an apology, and then said, "How's everything?"

From there on in, the scenario went pretty much as I'd imagined it—with one small exception: the part about the gloves. I don't know why I put that in anyway. I *never* wear gloves for show, only for warmth. And one big exception: the ending.

Right after Bart said, "You mean I'm never going to see you again?" he said "Don't go—you mustn't, yet! There's something I want to tell you."

I sat down.

"What is it?" I asked.

"Annie," he took my hand in his and looked into my eyes. "Annie, I'm in love. I know there's an awfully big difference in our ages, but I'm sure that's not an insurmountable problem."

Even with*out* my ESP he felt that way! I don't mind admitting I was enormously touched and flattered. And sorry for him—because nice and adorable as he was, it was Boris I really loved. If only he'd told me earlier, I might have been able to head him off.

"You certainly kept your feelings a secret. How long have you known?"

"Since Wednesday night." Wednesday night. The night of the blackout. I was crashing around in the dark with my mother, and Bart was—?

"Where were you Wednesday night?"

"At home," he rhapsodized. "In the flickering candlelight, sharing a loaf of bread, a jug of wine . . ." GIRL'S FACE SETS LUNCHROOM ON FIRE. How could I have *made* such a mistake!

"With whom," I asked. "I mean, what's her name?" As if I didn't know.

"Virginia. We met in the strangest way. It was as though it had been decreed by fate. I was on my way into the *Daily News* building, Tuesday afternoon—" That was the day I told Virginia it was all off between Bart and me. "—and she bumped into me and we got to talking and that's how it all began. She's the prettiest girl in the world. She has—"

"Honey-colored hair, blue eyes, a tiny top, and a tiny tummy, right?"

"Annie, were you lying to me before? It sounds as though you haven't lost your ESP at all."

"That wasn't ESP—it was just an educated guess."

I rose, slipped on my blue-jean jacket, and gracefully extended my hand. He took it, and shook it cordially.

"*Am* I ever going to see you again? What's your educated guess on that?"

"My educated guess is yes." (At the class dance. I'll be with Boris and you'll be with Virginia-the-Body-Snatcher.)

"Good-bye, Bartholomew," I said.

How *about* that Virginia!

Saturday afternoon, May 4

AT FIVE MINUTES TO FOUR, I was polishing Sascha's new dining-room table when Boris called to me.

"Annabel, put away the cleaning things and come here. I have a surprise for you."

"Where are you?"

"In the den," he shouted.

"What's the surprise? I don't see anything."

He pointed to the television set; it was on.

"You mean we're going to watch the Derby? That's not much of a surprise."

"No, but how about this?" From behind his back, he produced a chilled bottle of Dom Perignon and two chilled glasses.

"I thought a little celebration was in order."

He uncorked the champagne with a magnificent *pop,* and poured us each some bubbly.

"Here's to you and me and, most of all," he raised his glass high in the air, "to Ticker Tape!"

We clinked glasses and took a sip.

"Mmn," I said.

"How do you like it?" he asked.

"Not at all. How do you?"

"Not much," he admitted. "I guess it takes practice."

We both took another sip.

"You know what?" I said. "We forgot to toast Sascha, of all people."

"So we did. Better late than never, I always say. Here's to you and me and Ticker Tape and *Sascha*!"

We took another sip.

"And Ape Face." Sip.

"And your Mom and Dad." Sip.

"And Lord and Taylor, and OTB." Sip.

"And Virginia."

"Boris, I am not drinking to Virginia."

"No? I thought she was your best friend?"

"Was is correct."

"Oh well," he shrugged. "Here's to—uh—Hector." Sip.

"And Bart." Whoops!

"Who's that?"

"A cousin of mine from Duluth."

"I'm not drinking to people I don't know. If we start that, we'll finish the bottle before the race starts. Say, Annabel, do you feel anything?"

"Nope." I burped. "Nothing good, anyway. Do

you?"

"Nope. Here's to our late, lamented Box." Sip.

"And to its new owner, Granddaddy Clovis who's deaf as a post," I giggled.

". . . and they're off!" shouted the announcer. "It's Gobbledygook way out in front with a fast start, followed by Super Stupidity, and Illiopolis, Bernie Busch is in the number four position . . . with Ticker Tape bringing up the rear."

Boris and I exchanged smug glances and sipped placidly at our Dom Perignon.

". . . And coming up fast on the outside is Cafe Noir, with Gobbledygook still in the lead, Bernie Busch has dropped back to seventh place, wait a minute! Ticker Tape is making a try for it; man, look at that little horse go. Ticker Tape is now in fourth place . . ."

"Come on, Ticker Tape, baby, come on!" screamed Boris.

"Boris, what are you screaming for, you know he's going to win anyway—COME ON TICKER TAPE—atta baby!"

". . . Gobbledygook has dropped back to fifth position, Super Stupidity, the odds-on favorite, is now in first, followed by Illiopolis, Ticker Tape third . . . Ticker Tape has just overtaken Illiopolis, coming into the home stretch now . . . Super Stupidity first, Ticker Tape half a length behind him and gaining . . ."

"Boris, stop jumping up and down on the bed—it's

a new bed, you'll bust the springs—COME ON, TICKER TAPE!"

". . . They're neck and neck now . . . Ticker Tape drawing ahead of Stuper Supidity . . . and it's TICKER TAPE! Winner by half a length! *Man,* what a *race* that *was*!"

Boris and I fell back onto the bed, exhausted and hoarse from screaming.

"I know it sounds silly," he said, "but I've never seen anything so exciting in my life."

"Nor me."

"Can you imagine anyone betting on a horse called Super Stupidity?"

". . . they'll be posting the official running time. Wa-it a minute, folks, there seems to be something . . . They're announcing something over the loudspeaker . . ."

"Boris!"

"Shut up and listen."

"Ladies and gentlemen, Eddie O'Rourke, Super Stupidity's jockey, has filed a complaint against Ticker Tape's jockey, Bud Balducci. He says Balducci whipped his horse—whipped Super Stupidity, that is—causing him to flinch and lose ground in the final seconds of the race. There will be a few minutes while the judges review the tapes to determine whether or not this was the case. Meanwhile, we bring you a brief message from our sponsor."

"Oh my God! Annabel!"

"I know," I said. "Feel my hands, they're like ice."

Boris's were, too. It's a miracle we didn't stick to each other.

"Ladies and gentlemen, the judges of the Kentucky Derby have come to a decision. Judge Marion Beaufort will make the announcement."

"We regret to inform you that it is our unanimous opinion, based on careful review of the tapes, that the charges lodged against Mr. Balducci were justified. Ticker Tape is, thereby, disqualified, and the official winner of this year's Kentucky Derby is Super Stupidity, ridden by jockey Eddie O'Rourke."

The announcer came back and droned on. "Super Stupidity's owner, Mrs. Tweetie Twombley, is now making her way to the winner's circle. . . ."

I turned off the set and looked at Boris. He was the color of pureed peas.

All he kept saying, over and over again, was, "I think I'm going to throw up. I think I'm going to throw up."

"It's the champagne."

"It's not the champagne and you know it. I think I'm going to throw up."

"Then stop talking about it and *do* it," I said. "But don't do it in here—you'll ruin the new rug."

He stumbled to the bathroom, closed the door, and stumbled right back again.

"Did you?" I asked.

"No. I couldn't. I'm going to do something else."

"What?"

"Kill myself." He lurched to the window and peered down. I yanked him away (he was weak as a puppy) and threw him into a chair.

I didn't know what to do with him. He seemed hellbent on taking the plunge.

"Boris, I have an idea! Do you think there's the remotest possibility that OTB would give you your money back?"

"No," he said, and staggered to his feet. This time, I threw him back in the chair and planted a foot on his chest. Then I reached for the phone.

"You're wasting your time."

"I'm not calling OTB, I'm calling the police."

Quick as lightning, in a single, deft judo maneuver, he grabbed my foot, threw me off balance, and floored me.

"Sorry about that," he said, brushing his hands off, "but I had to stop you somehow. I'm going to my room."

"What for? So you can splash to your death right on Central Park West instead of in an empty courtyard? And possibly kill an innocent pedestrian as well as yourself?"

"I'm going to my room to pack. I'm running away."

I scrambled to my feet and followed him.

"That's the most cowardly thing I ever heard of. The least you could do is wait 'til Sascha comes back and tell her what you did and why you did it."

"I'd rather kill myself," he said, and began stuffing clothes into a Woolworth shopping bag.

"Here," he said, ripping a sheet of paper off his bulletin board. "Here's the itemized list I read to you—all nicely retyped. If you're so worried about Sascha, *you* tell her. Go over the list point by point. She probably won't know what you're talking about, but—"

"And what do I tell her when the bills come in? Boris, you can't do this to me."

As it turned out, he couldn't. Because just then, the doorbell rang.

"That's her!" I said.

"She," corrected Boris (about grammar, he's as bad as Virginia), and took a step toward the window. I blocked him. He sidestepped me. Once more, I blocked him. The doorbell rang again, longer and more persistently, this time, and was followed up by knocking and pounding.

"You answer it," he whispered. "While you're letting her in, I'll slip out the back door."

Out the window was more like it. I didn't dare leave him alone.

"No, Boris, I'm not taking any chances with you. Come on, we're both going to let her in."

I grabbed him by the arm and began dragging him to the front hall.

"Now listen, Boris. Put a good face on it. When we open the door, be smiling and happy to see her, and smiling and happy about how wonderful the place looks. Then, we'll show her around the apartment and show her her new clothes and then . . ." I faltered.

"And then what?" said Boris.

"And then she'll be in a marvelous mood and we'll tell her the rest."

"Oh . . . oh," he moaned. "I really think I'm going to throw up."

"No, you're not, I said firmly, although I wasn't too sure. He was no longer the color of pureed peas. He looked more like pureed eggplant—gray and seedy. I'd have to put a good face on my own face—Boris's was obviously a lost cause.

Sascha was now banging on the door with something hard—a shoe probably—and shouting, "Will somebody please let me in? I forgot my key!"

"Steady on, Boris, this is it."

With a radiant smile, I opened the door. Boris cowered behind it.

"Annabel!" she said, shifting her suitcase to the other hand and shaking mine. "What a delight!"

"Hello, Mrs. . . . Sascha. Come in."

She hesitated. "Only for a minute. I can't stay long."

Then, apparently baffled, she said, "I wonder why Hector let me off here?"

What is she talking about? Oh, now I see. Everything looks so different, she thinks she's in my apartment. This was going to be a lark. (The first part, anyway.)

"Because you live here," I said airily.

Sascha winked at me, and in a tone of mock wonderment said, "I *do*? Funny—it doesn't look at all the way it did when I left."

"Of course not. It's been done over. Welcome home."

Boris crept out from behind the door with his shopping bag. "Welcome home, Sascha," he echoed feebly.

"Hi there, friend. I didn't expect to see you here."

"I live here, too, remember?"

Sascha laughed. "Listen, fellas, the joke's over. I may be unobservant but I'm not that unobservant. I know my own home when I see it. . . . Boris, what are you doing with that shopping bag full of clothes?"

"I'm taking a trip," he said, inching toward the door.

She clearly didn't believe that either. "I can't say much for your luggage. To what unchic place are you going, might I ask?"

"No place," I said, blocking his way.

"Well, *I* am," said Sascha. "I'm going to *my* unchic

place and take a hot bath."

I decided it was time to get the show on the road.

"Sascha, you're in it. You can take a bath right here. This *is* your home. It's not a joke."

She set her suitcase down and looked around. "No? What is it, then?"

"It's a surprise. While you were away, Boris had the apartment painted and we got new furniture and new clothes for you. . . ."

She turned to Boris. "True?" she asked. He managed a faint smile—actually, more of a grimace—and nodded.

"That's quite a surprise," she said expressionlessly.

"Come on, Boris," I said, pulling him away from the door. "Let's give her the Fifty-Cent Tour." An unfortunate phrase, but it was out of my mouth before I realized it.

The Fifty-Cent Tour was conducted entirely by me. Boris, an ambulatory zombie, contributed not one word and neither did Sascha. I felt like a showroom salesman with a couple of obdurate clients.

"Well," I said heartily, when we were back in the entrance hall, "how does it grab you?"

"I haven't decided yet," said Sascha.

Boris had finally found his voice—some of it, anyway. In a tentative croak, he said, "How about the paint job? Isn't it nice?"

"For a men's washroom, or an intensive care unit at

Bellevue, very nice."

Then she pointed to the new white Naugahyde living-room sofa, and said, "Is it permitted to sit down on that? Because if so, I would like to sit there with both of you until I find out what this is all about."

We arranged ourselves, Sascha in the middle and Boris and me on either side. "All right," she said quietly, "what *is* it all about?"

"Well, Sascha." Boris had now recovered the rest of his voice and it was coming out loud and clear and, I'm afraid, pompous. "For some time, now, I've been dissatisfied with the way things have been going around here."

"Indeed," she said. "Would you care to elucidate?"

Boris would. And for ten uninterrupted minutes, he did. It was as though years of pent-up indignation were finally exploding out of him. He told her what he thought of her as a housekeeper—rotten; as a manager of financial matters—careless and irresponsible; as a wife—a failure, obviously, or Pop wouldn't have eft her; as a mother—inadequate; and as a human being—talented, but disorganized, self-destructive, unhappy, and badly in need of making a fresh start in life but utterly incapable of doing it on her own.

"So you've decided to help me, is that it, Boris?!"

"That's it," he said.

Aside from the whirring of the new digital clock, the silence in the room was deafening.

"And according to you, a fresh start in life begins with a fresh coat of paint."

"Yes. It's only a beginning, of course, but I felt there's nothing like new surroundings to turn a person's head around."

"You have definitely turned mine around. In fact, I'm amazed it's still attached to my neck," she said acidly. "This fresh start you're going to help me make—is it for me or is it for you?"

"For both of us, but primarily for you."

"In that case, don't you think you might have consulted me before you embarked on it? How do you know I want to make one?"

"I'm sure you don't," he said. "I don't mean to be rude, Sascha, but people like you always hate letting go of their hang-ups."

She smiled pleasantly at him; but I sensed something menacing underneath the smile. There was enough electricity in the room to light up Times Square, although Boris seemed blissfully unaware of it.

"I certainly hate letting go of my wonderful, battered old desk and my squooshy couch, my Peruvian rug, and all the other lares and penates you've seen fit to dispose of—if that's what you mean by hang-ups.

"But of course," she said sarcastically, "you know what's best for me, don't you, Boris? You know what will make me happy."

Boris shifted uncomfortably.

"Has it never passed through that conservative, Naugahyde-bound, mingy little mind of yours that I already *am* happy?"

Boris shifted again. "I think you *think* you're happy."

"Would you like to know what I think of what you think? Get a load of this, Mac!"

She picked up a brand-new brass lamp (seventy-five bucks) and threw it at the brand-new stainless-steel-and-glass coffee table (three hundred bucks). Smithereen time.

Boris winced. I winced. Sascha scornfully kicked the shards out of her way and went on.

"You want to make me over in your own image, don't you? What's best for Boris is best for Sascha, right? WRONG! What's best for Boris is only best for Boris. I *like* the way I am, and believe it or not, so do quite a few other people. As a matter of fact even your father liked me."

Boris looked startled.

"That shocks you, doesn't it? Judging by what you said before, I knew it would. It seems you have been laboring under a misapprehension, Mr. Fixit. Your father left me only because after years of trying to reconcile the basic differences in our personalities, *I* was convinced that we were hopelessly mismatched, and *I* finally persuaded him to go."

She paused for a moment, looked at Boris, and in a gentler, more reflective tone, continued. "I am a rotten housekeeper—no doubt about it. I can't help it, or else I don't want to help it, because those things just aren't important to me. I spent my entire childhood with a mother to whom food and furnishings mattered terribly, and I swore, when I grew up, that I wouldn't let them matter to me. I never wanted the kind of house where a kid couldn't climb on a couch.

"As for my lack of business acumen, Boris, that's baloney. Since when haven't you had enough to eat? Since when, enough to wear? Since when, a private school? We've always survived, haven't we? Maybe not your way—but your way is not my way.

"Now, let's talk about me as a mother."

"Let's not," said Boris in a quavering voice. On the verge of tears, he was pop-eyed from trying to hold them back.

Sascha ignored him. "Inadequate, you say. Well, if you say so, then it's true; because if that's how I seem to *you,* then that's what I am. And I'm truly sorry. We've always been on different wavelengths, I guess.

"But Boris, how about a little respect for someone else's wavelength? You happen to be clearheaded, disciplined, conventional, and extremely bright. I accept you the way you are. I, on the other hand, happen to be muddleheaded, self-indulgent, a confirmed nut, and a pretty good writer. Can't you accept me the way *I* am?"

"I *do,* Sasch." Boris was losing the battle of the tears.

"No, you don't," she said flatly. "I'm always aware of your disapproval. You don't bother to disguise it very well. Living with you is like living with a German governess. You know something? I've been afraid of you for years now. Isn't that ludicrous—for a mother to be afraid of her own son?!"

Boris was openly sobbing now.

"But Sasch, I'm afraid of you, too. You'll think it's stuffy and boring of me, but I never know what's coming next. I never know what you're going to do, where you're going to be—everything is always so uncertain."

"*Everything,* friend? At least you know I love you—you're not uncertain about that, are you?"

Boris evidently was. He looked up at her, his eyes full of tears and doubt.

"Because I do, baby, I do."

Then with a great shuddering sigh, he put his head in her lap.

"I love you, too, Sasch."

I started to leave.

Sascha said, "You don't have to go, Annabel. It's only fireworks. Good, healthy fireworks. We should have had them long ago."

"Sascha," whispered Boris, "I've done something awful. On this stupid apartment that doesn't even matter to you, I've spent over twelve thousand dollars of your money. I thought I was going to get it all back and more, betting on a horse, but the bloody horse lost. Now what are we going to do?"

She smoothed back his hair, and with the corner of her silk blouse wiped away the tears.

"Do? We're going to take some of the fifty thousand dollars Paramount just gave me for writing a movie script, and pay up—that's what we're going to do."

Boris was a new man. "Oh wow, what a relief!"

"Knowing you, I'm sure it is—but Boris, my angel, if I hadn't made that money, we would have survived anyway. We always do. When are you going to realize that?"

He blinked. You could almost see the light bulb going on in his head. "Right now!" he said joyfully. "And I'm never going to forget it."

"Oh yes you will," she said with a laugh. "That's the way you are—a born pessimist. Don't worry—I'm used to it. I forgive you in advance. However, there's just one thing . . ." She paused. "One thing I want to ask of you. If you wouldn't mind."

"Get the walls repainted."

"Hell no!" said Sascha. "Normal wear and tear around here will take care of the walls. They'll be gray in two months. No, it's . . ." she paused again. Whatever she wanted to say was apparently awkward.

“I’ll do anything, Sascha, just name it.”

“Okay, then, here it is: I wish you wouldn’t call me Sascha. That’s for everybody else to call me. (Except my father who still calls me Sarah.) But there’s only one person in the whole world who can call me Mom.”

She looked at him, kind of embarrassed. But Boris grinned at her, not a bit embarrassed. “Sure, Mom. Be glad to. I never liked the name Sascha anyway.”

I do, I thought. I love the name Sascha because I love her. Just the way I love the name Boris (which is a dumb name really, even dumber than Morris) because I love him. More now than ever before. In fact, right now, I love everybody. Even Virginia!

This is not the end. Please turn the page and read carefully. Then decide what you think.

Barron University
Dept. of ESP and Parapsychology
Greensboro, N.C.

Ms. Annabel Andrews
115 C.P.W.
N.Y., N.Y., 10023

Dear Ms. Andrews,

This is to acknowledge receipt of your manuscript and to thank you for sending it. My colleagues and I found it extremely provocative; in fact, we wonder if there might be a way to document the account by means of concrete evidence. In other words, could you give us the exact name and address of your housekeeper's Granddaddy Clovis? Since he is hard of hearing, the Box cannot be of any significant value to him; surely a larger, more recent model would please him just as well. An exchange such as this would be beneficial to both parties; we are, therefore, anxious to communicate with Granddaddy Clovis as soon as possible.

As for your highly commendable concern that the Box not be misused for purposes of personal gain, I wish to alleviate any fears you may have regarding this: We, here at the University, are interested in the Box only insofar as it will aid us in our altruistic quest for knowledge. (Admittedly, we *would* like to know in advance how our report on the latest ESP findings will be received by the public when we present it next month, because a large grant rests on the outcome; but I promise you, we have no interest in horse racing.)

Looking forward to hearing from you soon, I remain

Yours very sincerely,
Oliver Elmswood.

P.S. My wife, who is a member of the English Department here, has also read your manuscript. Although I am convinced she is wrong, she tends to regard it as fiction and recommends that you send it to her old friend, Ursula Nordstrom, Senior Editor at Harper & Row. In the unlikely event that my wife's assessment of the manuscript is accurate, I am passing this information on to you; however, please note the enclosed stamped, self-addressed envelope, in which I fully expect to receive your information on the whereabouts of Granddaddy Clovis.

O. E.